To my f[?]
Pat

THE JETHART HOUSE

Alex Ferguson

Also by this author

Maggie Magee and the Last Magician
Village Life
The Time Walkers
A Most Peculiar Hotel
Fields Of Stone
Tiggie
The Pineapple King Of Jarrow
Uncle Freddie & The Prince Of Wales

THE JETHART HOUSE

A Ravelled Tale of Murder and Betrayal,
Of Good and Evil

Alex Ferguson

ISBN: 978-0-244-97764-1

PublishNation
www.publishnation.co.uk

ALEX FERGUSON is a national award-winning writer with Silver and Gold Awards from the Writers' Guild. He worked with Corin and Vanessa Redgrave to write three successful plays for Moving Theatre. THE FLAG was performed at Battersea & CASEMENT at the Riverside. He has contributed to a number of television series and built a successful reputation in radio and theatre drama. His comic radio series ran for six years on Radio Four. He created and ran the youth theatre company, Bold As Brass, on Tyneside for ten years which climaxed in a wonderful run at the Jermyn Street Theatre with DO YOU SEE WHAT I SEE? In 2016 he wrote the feature film, BLISS! which has been chosen for screening by four International Film Festivals in the United Kingdom, Europe and the United States. Tiring of chasing actors to perform, he sat down to write books and filled a shelf on Kindle.

The Golden Rule:

Do not confuse the Reality with the Manifestation

BEGINNING

When Detective Constable Susan Jobling views a CCTV tape from a Newcastle charity shop she is both startled and amazed by what she sees. No one at her station can be bothered to look at the tape. Sadly, this bright young woman's nickname at this chauvinistic station is Duff Job and the visit to investigate a burglary at the charity shop is typical of the duff jobs she is assigned.

But when two teenagers disappear in very disturbing circumstances after visiting the Queen's House in the ancient town of Jedburgh, Sally recognises the link between the videotape and the Jethart House. She has stumbled upon a deadly mystery that surmounts time. The young detective learns ours is not a singular universe and perseveres despite the ridicule of the chauvinists. Too many people are dying for no apparent reason. Sally pursues the psychopathic villain who moves through time to kill all in his path who would reveal the truth of an age-old mystery.

In my ending is my beginning, as the ill-fated Scottish Queen, Mary Stuart wrote. In the ending of this remarkable story is the beginning of something most extraordinary.

Alex Ferguson

ONE

The decapitated head of the old woman, trailing threads of blood, rolled slowly across the floor and stopped in front of Paul. The head rocked on the uneven flagstones as the teenager struggled to breathe. The eyes looked upwards beseechingly at Paul who could not tear his gaze from the flickering eyelids. When the mouth said, "Don't forget your packed lunch," the teenager screamed and woke up.

In the silence of his familiar room Paul lay unmoving, heart pounding, but immensely relieved, grateful for the volume of noise from the bathroom next door where his twin sister Amy sang and showered. His head bumped against the book on his pillow: Antonia Fraser's Mary Queen of Scots.

"Thanks a heap, Antonia," Paul said aloud and dropped the book to the floor.

When he swung his feet to the Mickey Mouse mat, the alarm clock began to buzz. He took an especial delight in slapping it into silence. Knuckles rapped on the door and his mother's voice declaimed, "Are you vertical, Paul, or shall I come in and embarrass you?"

In the bathroom, the shower and singing stopped.

"I'm up, Mum, I'm up," Paul declared and reached for his dressing gown.

"You don't want to miss the coach, do you?" coaxed the voice from the landing.

Don't I? thought Paul, *I wouldn't bet on it.*

When he opened the bedroom door his mother was retreating down the stairs and the bathroom door stood open. Paul entered and showered the nightmare out of his head.

*

3

When Paul arrived in the kitchen a large ginger cat strolled forward to block his passage, refusing to give way until he bent to stroke its amiable head.

"Get any bigger, and you'll burst," Paul decided.

"Charming," said Amy, already at the table eating toast.

"Not you, Skinny Lizzie."

His mother was bustling to and fro. That's what she does, thought Paul, she's a bustler.

"You used my shampoo," Amy said, reaching for the last of the toast.

"No, I didn't," countered Paul.

"I can smell it. Don't bother to lie."

"Only a drop left in the bottle," Paul confessed.

"Not now there isn't," said Amy.

Paul's mother placed a plate of egg, sausage, bacon and fried bread under his nose.

"Thanks, Mum."

"And you will buy your sister shampoo?"

"Yes, Mum."

"How you can swallow all that this time of a morning," Amy reflected.

"Me man," Paul explained, "You girl. Girl want big eyelashes. Me want big muscles."

"You get big belly," said Amy and laughed.

Joyce Bowman poured tea for Paul, refilled her own cup and regarded Paul affectionately.

"The handsomest of the Bowmans."

"Hey!" Amy complained, "What about me?"

"I said handsomest. I didn't say most beautiful," and stroked her daughter's hair.

She drained her tea and rose, saying, "Love you and leave you. Meetings all day. Enjoy the trip to Jedburgh. I remember the house where Mary Queen of Scots lived."

Amy said, "She didn't live there. She was on a visit when she fell ill."

"You could've sorted that, Mum," Paul suggested, "No leeches. No bleeding. Just a course of antibiotics."

Doctor Bowman laughed.

Aren't I lucky, she thought, *to have such children?*

"See you this evening," she decided, "But be good!"

Amy protested, "We're always good."

"Not according to Mrs. Balfour."

"Teachers don't understand us," said Paul.

"Or they understand you too well?" his mother suggested.

"They don't understand how we communicate," Amy explained, "We don't need mobiles. We just know"

"What we're both thinking," Paul said, "And they don't like it."

"Miss Probert says we're sly. Which is sad because she's really quite nice."

"Why have you never told me this?"

"What does it matter?" said Paul, "We're the Terrible Twins."

"Don't worry about it," Amy said, "We'll be especially well behaved today."

"We won't answer the question before she's finished asking it," Paul suggested. "And you be careful too, Mum," Amy warned, "The Connellys blame you for what happened."

"They have a right to their opinion."

"But not to threaten to kill you."

"That's despicable," Amy agreed.

"They're all hot air," their mother assured them, "I don't take them seriously."

Joyce Bowman kissed both her children and headed for the kitchen door.

"Don't forget your packed lunch," she said and vanished.

*

"I'll tell you something you don't know," suggested Amy.

"Such as?"

"After Mary was executed the body moved and everyone was absolutely terrified."

"Do I need to know this?"

"Then a little lap dog struggled out from under her robe."

"And everybody fell about laughing?"

Amy regarded her brother sternly.

"You're not taking this seriously."

Paul grimaced to say, "I'm trying not to. But she wasn't executed at Jedburgh. That was years later at Fotheringhay. But I'll tell you something you should know."

"Go on!"

"We share the same birthday, Her Majesty and us. Spooky, eh?"

Amy said, solemnly, "I don't think we'll tell Miss Probert. She'll say we're swanking."

They regarded one another, auburn hair, hazel eyes, tall for their age, mirror images in neat school uniform, inseparable from conception, the Bowman twins.

"Do we have to go to Jedburgh?" Paul suggested.

Amy joked, "You mean absent ourselves from an educational outing without written permission risking the possibility of spending the rest of our lives in detention supervised by Miss Probert?"

Paul laughed.

"It's not like digging out from Colditz."

"We're going to Jedburgh," Amy determined, "Mum's made up our lunch boxes.

You've got that disgusting salami."

She handed her brother his lunch box, which he stuffed roughly into his shabby haversack. Amy lamented, "Why does Mum bother to make you up a nice lunch when you do that?"

"Okay, we'll go," Paul decided, "But don't say I didn't warn you. It'll be totally dead boring."

*

Outside the gates of the William Woodhave Comprehensive School, the A Level History group foregathered, awaiting the arrival of the coach. A young and insecure Miss Probert counted and recounted her group, worried about the arrival, non-arrival of the coach and constantly checked her watch. When the Bowman twins arrived to bid her good morning politely, she released some of her accumulated tension by turning upon them.

"Ah, the Bowman twins!" Miss Probert declaimed, "So good of you to join us!"

The twins almost looked at one another. This barely discernible communication irritated the teacher further despite the sycophantic laughter of her inner group.

"Weren't you expecting us, miss?" asked Paul innocently.

Miss Probert ignored him to consult her clipboard yet again.

"Aren't we on the list, miss?" Amy enquired.

"Can't you see I'm busy?" countered Miss Probert.

"Sorry, miss."

Paul signalled disappointment to Amy who laughed irritating Miss Probert further.

"Unless you'd prefer to go into school?" enquired Miss Probert archly.

"No, miss," Amy responded brightly, "We've been looking forward to going for simply ages."

At which Paul struggled to turn laughter into coughing.

*

Detective Constable Susan Duffy parked the police car on the restricted zone outside William Woodhave Comprehensive School and wound down the window.

The chatter of schoolchildren filled the car as a racket of starlings.

"The happiest days of your life. So they tell us."

Police Cadet John Timothy, in the passenger seat, said, "I enjoyed school."

Susan gave the gawky, ginger-headed young man a disapproving glance and he defended himself, saying, "So this is detective work? Sitting outside a school in a car with POLICE all over it?"

A car slowed down to park, but the driver changed her mind on seeing the police car and drove on.

"The school," said Susan, "has complained about parent parking."

"But while we're sitting here, they won't!"

"Exactly."

"But wouldn't a traffic warden or a C.S do as well?"

Susan said, "Ours not to reason why. Ours but to waste our time."

The cadet sighed, "They must think I'm useless."

When Susan looked at him, he added hastily, "Not you. Two commendations. I looked you up."

Susan thought, *Duff job? Give it to Duffy.*

Aloud she said, "So what did you like about school?"

*

Swarms of envious youngsters paused to ask where the History group was going. At the gates Mr. Buckley waited to check whether they were suitably clad for another day's imprisonment. The girls rolled down their skirts to the required length while the boys tucked in their shirts. Both sexes adjusted ties and enjoyed a last frantic chewing of the cud before casting precious gum to the ground. The pavement outside the gates of William Woodhave Comp was liberally carpeted with chewing gum.

The most reluctant of the reluctant scholars passed scrutiny. Mr. Buckley closed the gates and retreated to the grey cliff of the school without a word to the exiled Miss Probert. Mr. Buckley didn't approve of "field trips". The History group was becoming restless and Miss Probert increasingly anxious before the coach finally appeared to the cheers of the History group.

"What time do you call this?" demanded Miss Probert.

The driver, a middle-aged, amiable man, obligingly tilted his cuff.

"I make it nine twenty-three, miss," but the teacher didn't miss the smile that passed between the twins as they boarded the coach. They were amused by the driver's notice: Please don't sing. I'm a music lover.

As the coach moved off D.C. Susan Duffy said, "Okay! That's us done," and started the engine. The cadet consulted his watch and dutifully noted the time on the log. Susan smiled.

"What's next?"

Susan said, "Vandalism. Corner shop."

The cadet cheered up visibly. Susan followed the coach long enough to make the driver nervous before overtaking and leaving it far

*

As the coach climbed steadily up to Carter Bar the pleading began.

"Please, miss, can we stop at the border?"

"Please, miss, I've promised me Mam a picture of me at the stone."

"Please, miss, I feel sick."

"Please, miss, we always stop at the border."

"Please, miss, I'm going to be sick."

Paul and Amy sat silent, studying their project folders, which somehow disappointed Miss Probert. When the pleading increased to a clamour, she stood up to declare, "We are not stopping at Carter Bar. Perhaps we may stop on the way home, but we need to press on to Jedburgh. We have an appointment with our guide at the House."

The pleading dwindled to a dismal grumble that grew louder as the summit appeared.

*

D.C. Susan Duffy parked the car outside the corner shop. Before she and the cadet exited the car the Asian shopkeeper and a teenage boy appeared on the pavement.

They had been awaiting their arrival.

Susan put on her best smile and approached the shopkeeper.

"Good morning, Mr. Patel!"

"We were expecting the police."

"Well, we're here now," said Susan.

"I had expected there would be a policeman."

Susan said, brightly, "I am Detective Constable Duffy and this is Cadet Timothy."

The shopkeeper regarded her with suspicion.

"A woman detective?"

Susan suppressed her instinctive response and asked, "What is the problem, Mr. Patel?"

She wore the solemn face she reserved for serious crime.

The shopkeeper said, "Someone has spat on my window!"

The Detective Constable and the Police Cadet stared at the plate glass. The shopkeeper was correct. Someone had spat on the window.

"And that is the problem, Mr. Patel?" Susan asked.

"Is that not enough?"

"What do you expect us to do about it?"

"Do about it?"

Mr. Patel was amazed.

"Surely there is enough DNA to identify the scoundrel?"

Susan returned to the passenger door of the car and opened the glove compartment.

"Is there any other damage?" Cadet Timothy asked brightly.

Detective Constable Duffy returned with an ice-lolly stick and a plastic envelope that had contained a football card. The cadet scraped some of the deposit from the window and dropped the stick into the plastic envelope. He placed the envelope in his breast tunic pocket. Mr. Patel was satisfied. He beamed upon the cadet.

Susan said, "As soon as we have a positive identification, we'll be in touch."

The cadet saluted smartly and leaving one satisfied customer behind, the police officers returned to the car with the vital evidence. As the car moved off the teenage boy stepped forward to wash the window.

"What next?" the cadet asked.

"Break-in and robbery at a charity shop."

"Somebody robbed a charity shop?"

Duff job? Give it to Duffy!

*

To Miss Probert's displeasure and the History Group's delight the coach pulled in beyond the border stone and stopped. The driver opened the door and a fresh Cheviot breeze filled the coach. Before the teacher could voice a protest the driver declared, "Ten minutes, mind yi! Or I'll leave yis behind!"

The Group tumbled out of the coach, thanking the driver who muttered, "Aye, aye, aye! Save it 'til I get yi home! If I get yi home!"

As the students took photographs of each other pointing at the word SCOTLAND or peeping from behind the stone, Miss Probert stormed down the coach, spluttering, "How dare you contradict me! I want your name, the name of your superior! And his telephone number! I'll make sure you never drive another coach for this school!"

Paul and Amy sat silent, heads down.

Why didn't we get out?

Because we're being well behaved.

If this is what well behaved does. She'll murder us for nothing. I'm going to get under the seat.

No, you're not!

Then I'm going to hold my breath until I die. Just sit still and scribble!

Scribble what?

Anything!

The driver said, "Don't talk so daft, lass! Just listen a minute. I've done yi a favour."

As Miss Probert's mouth opened to respond, Amy's pencil fell to the floor and rolled down the coach.

Brilliant move, sis!

I didn't do it on purpose!

Miss Probert became aware the Bowman twins were on the coach. She turned to glare at their silent, downcast, shampooed, auburn heads.

The driver said, "If we didn't stop, yi'd've made a miserable day for yasel. Before yi even got started. Give them ten minutes. Keep them happy!"

Miss Probert called up the coach, "You two! Out!"

Reluctantly, Paul and Amy rose to exit the coach, straining not to look at the teacher.

*

The bell rang shrilly as Susan Duffy and the cadet entered the charity shop, breathing in the mixture of decay, damp, soap powder and unrealised hope that inhabits such premises. The racks were full of discarded clothing, the shelves stuffed with yellowing paperbacks and videotapes no one would ever read or watch again. An optimistic old man checked the pockets of jackets on the racks and a young woman with a baby in her arms riffled through the tee shirts. The unspoken question in the eyes of Cadet Timothy when he looked at the detective constable was: *who on earth would want to steal this junk?*

As they advanced through the shop, a brisk, middle-aged woman came from the rear premises and answered the unspoken question.

"I'm sure you're finding it difficult to believe anyone would wish to rob our shop," she declared, "We're not Oxfam. Or Cancer Research. You wouldn't know you were in a charity shop with them. We're just Saint Jude's. I'm afraid we're not the first choice for donations."

In one hand she held a cardigan of bilious hue and in the other a mournful rabbit with one ear.

"Detective Constable Duffy," Susan announced, "Police Cadet Timothy. And you are?"

"Missis Brannigan. But do call me Molly."

For one moment Susan was tempted to ask the rabbit's name.

"And you manage the shop?"

"Yes."

"Could you tell us, Molly, what exactly has been stolen?"

From her apron pocket Molly Brannigan unfolded a sheet of paper.

Why on earth would she keep a record of this junk?

"Dwayne and I have just finished stocktaking. So it wasn't difficult."

"Dwayne?" asked the cadet.

"My right hand man," and then mistaking the cadet's intention, "No, no, a very decent young man. One can't judge by appearances. He pays for everything. He's into vinyl records."

Molly Brannigan waited until Cadet Timothy finished his note taking and then read from her list.

"Two men's polo neck jumpers. One navy blue. One grey. One pair leather trousers. One leather jacket. One pair cowboy boots. Size thirteen. That's why they were still here. Size thirteen."

The cadet patiently compiled his list.

Susan said, "If I had wanted to buy that lot, how much would it have cost?"

Molly Brannigan said wistfully, "Would fifteen pounds be too much?"

"Were they in good nick?"

"They belonged to a taxi driver. His brother brought them in. He was run over by his brother's taxi."

"Twenty quid," decided Susan.

"People do tend to haggle," Molly said.

The cadet said, "So we're looking for a big man dressed like a taxi driver."

"What damage was done?" Susan queried, "Front door? Rear window?"

"Oh, no," said Molly, "They didn't damage anything."

"They?" said the young detective constable, "How do you know they?"

"Would you like to see our CCTV?"

Reluctantly Susan nodded agreement.

"Why not?"

TWO

Susan quickly realised Dwayne was a resourceful young man. It was a neat package with two motion-sensitive cameras covering the shop.

"I've reeled it back to where they come in," Molly explained and switched on the tape.

There was movement outside the door of the charity shop. There appeared to be a child and a big man crouched at the door.

Molly said, "He's picking the lock. My father always said locks only stopped honest men."

To Susan and the cadet's amazement a man and a dwarf in fancy dress entered the shop and carefully closed the door behind them. They appeared to be dressed in historical fashion. The big man wore cloak, doublet and hose with a sword belted about his waist. He was bearded and showed no concern about cameras. His companion, the dwarf, was dressed in a mail coat, belted with a sword, an iron cap and carried a cross bow. A quiver of bolts hung between his shoulders.

"I don't believe it," the cadet said, "It's a joke!"

Susan gestured him to silence. The dwarf capered about the shop, posing in women's hats and scarves, poking his nose into everything and throwing garments about. The big man worked steadily through the racks, choosing carefully. Susan noted that he collected the sweaters, jacket and trousers measuring them against himself casually, but he sat down to try on the cowboy boots.

"It's no joke," said Susan.

As if he heard her speak, the big man looked up into the camera. It was a face that frightened Susan, a strong, cold face, black-bearded, the face of a violent man. As they watched, the big man picked up his choice of clothing and headed for the shop door, followed by the dwarf who pushed over clothes racks as he went, exiting the shop in a feather boa with a baseball cap on his helmet.

Molly Brannigan switched off the video player and the trio sat silent in the rear room of the charity shop.

Susan said slowly, "I think these two men are very dangerous."

Realising what she'd said, Susan added, "But they're not going to bother you again, Molly. They have what they came for. D'y'think I could have the tape?"

Susan and the cadet were silent as they drove back to the station, but Susan could not erase the face of the big man from her mind.

*

"Wha'd'y'think, sir?" said Detective Constable Duffy.

D.I. Harold Starling didn't look up from the file he was reading.

"About what?"

"The video tape from the charity shop."

"How much was the gear worth they nicked?"

"Fifteen quid. Mebbes twenty?"

"Waste of time."

The Inspector's attention returned to his file.

"Could I have the tape, sir?"

"No way. It's in the system now."

The videotape lay in the Out tray. The D.I. looked up from his file.

"Anything else?"

Susan shook her head.

"Then buzz off! Some of us has work to do."

*

The twins stood in the morning sunlight looking across at the Muckle Cheviot: the sky populated with the most innocent of cotton wool clouds. They didn't need to say a single word. The beauty of the morning created a frisson of joy that chimed throughout their being.

"I bet," said Paul, "this was a nightmare in the winter. Can you imagine trying to bring horses and wagons over this summit in a snow storm?"

The playground chatter of the Group was interrupted by Miss Probert.

"Come along! You've had more than ten minutes! Let's not waste any more time!"

As the Group boarded the coach the twins approached reluctantly.

"Don't look at the Gorgon," Paul whispered, "Or she'll turn us to stone," which didn't help. Amy laughed as she climbed aboard.

The Gorgon gave the twins a glacial glare, but they reached their seats in the rear of the coach unscathed.

"Now, driver," suggested Miss Probert, "May we proceed to Jedburgh?"

The coach pulled out and began the long descent into Scotland and the little town called Jedburgh where once a sad Queen came to visit.

*

In bedroom Number Seven of the Old Manse, Jesmond Road, Jedburgh, a distinguished three-storey detached house, Margaret Lennox, a middle-aged woman of undistinguished appearance, was making the bed. Number Seven was the premier room in what Mrs. Lennox called her Family Hotel. It was most definitely not a Bed & Breakfast like numbers seventeen and twenty-three, but a Family Hotel for the Discerning as per the discreet board at the gate. Every room offered a king-size double bed, Sky television and tea maker.

Margaret Lennox was putting the finishing touches to Number Seven in preparation for the arrival of Mr. Fullerton from St. John's, Oxford when she felt a faint tremor, a slight palpitation of the heart. She stood still for a moment awaiting the echo to repeat, but there was nothing. Her body and the house were silent. She looked to her cat curled undisturbed in the window seat. Under her gaze the cat looked up and mewed softly, rebuking her excitement.

"I know, I know! I'm a foolish old woman, but he is my favourite guest. A flutter of the heart, maybe?"

Margaret Lennox was dressing Number Seven for Mr. Fullerton with cotton sheets and a counterpane fresh from the dry cleaner. No nylon sheets or cheap duvet for Mr. Fullerton. Nothing but Egyptian cotton and duck down were good enough. She smiled to herself in anticipation of a pleasant evening spent in the company of a cultured gentleman. She would find in the cellar another bottle of the burgundy he had much enjoyed on his last visit. They were becoming such good friends. There had even been a hint of an invitation to his College, dinner at High Table, on the last but one visit, but nothing since.

Margaret Lennox had picked up her cat and stopped at the door to inspect the bedroom when at the very edge of perception something touched a thread of the web. Long, long ago, almost beyond memory she had felt such an alarum.

When the travelling show had come to Priory Meadow. But that was so long ago. Margaret Lennox smiled at her foolishness and retreated to the kitchen.

*

The coach bearing the History Group turned off from the A68 and entered the little town of Jedburgh, passing the first or last shop in Scotland, the rugby ground, and bumped over the bridge as Miss Probert struggled to keep the students in their seats.

"Miss, miss, can we have our dinners now? We're starving!"

"No, we will not have lunch now. We're late for our appointment at the House.

We'll go there first to apologise to the Curator. We'll have lunch when I say so."

The grumbling subsided, but like the uneasy sea was not at rest. Paul and Amy sat peacefully in their seats being well behaved.

*

Preparing vegetables at the kitchen sink, Margaret Lennox saw the coach bearing the school party pass the Old Manse. Then the web jangled violently and the knife slipped to cut her finger. Sucking at the wound, she listened and the pain began in her breast just as it had so many, many years before when the travelling show came to Priory Meadow.

Her hands had burned like hot irons as she lifted the twin babes from the basket in the caravan and drowned them in the Jedwater. The baby girl had died so easily under her foot, drowning almost without protest, bubbling into death, but the boy had almost slipped from her

17

grasp forcing her to kneel on his chest, the river water lapping her chin. When she was sure both children were dead Margaret Lennox let the Jedwater carry the corpses away from her.

For a long moment with the current tugging at her gown, she had remained on her knees, chin-deep in the water, listening to the night sounds of the river and the echo of music from the Meadow. Then she had returned to the brothel where one of the men awaiting her attention was the father of the dead twins.

Abandoning the vegetables and Mr. Fullerton, bulldog of St. John's, Oxford, Margaret Lennox bustled into her coat and fled the Old Manse.

From the lane corner, the witch watched the teenagers disembark from the coach under the anxious supervision of the teacher. She waited while the teacher spoke shortly to the coach driver and then set off for the Queen's House, followed by the A Level History group, laughing and larking.

Following at a discreet distance, Margaret Lennox sniffed the air, listening and tasting, struggling to differentiate one scent from the confusion of so many. In the tourist bustle of the High Street the alien scent dwindled and was lost in the confusion of so many odours. But still the web vibrated and her mortal body was racked with such pain she stopped to rest against a pillar-box, fighting for breath.

A woman coming out of the baker's shop recognised her.

"Margaret," she enquired, "Are you alright, dear?"

Margaret Lennox struggled to remember the woman's name.

"I'm fine, Annie, I'm fine."

"I must say you don't look it, dear."

Grasping at straws, Margaret Lennox explained, "It's these shoes. I should have more sense at my age. They're giving me fair gyp!"

The puzzled expression on the woman's face made Margaret Lennox look down at her feet. She was wearing bedroom slippers. The woman called Annie walked away, shoulders stiff with offence.

The scent was lost, but the witch knew where the school party was going. When the pain subsided to an endurable level she made her way to the Jethart House. When she reached the garden railings of the House she saw the Gemini and her breast roared again with pain. But the witch could not enter the garden.

Margaret Lennox had watched and waited many lifetimes, in many guises, here where the fabric of time was ruptured in Jethart: the little town where the folly of the Queen of Scots might be overthrown. When the House had fallen into disrepair, Margaret Lennox had rejoiced. When the House was restored to its former glory she despaired. But here she waited in changing times from bothie to pothouse to corn merchant to milliner to chandler to chemist to brothel keeper and abortionist to housekeeper to B&B to Family Hotel for the Discerning, listening for the trembling of the web. Now the coming of the Gemini threatened to untangle the tragic history of a sad Queen.

*

The A Level History group entered the grounds of the Queen's House chattering like starlings despite the best efforts of Miss Probert to silence her students. Yet even the most wilful of the party fell silent as they entered the ancient portal and gathered under the barrel roof of the guard chamber to meet the Custodian, a bright sparrow of a woman, who smiled upon the teenagers as if she had been waiting a lifetime to meet them: which proportionately she had been.

"Hello!" she began brightly, "My name is Mary MacDonald and it's my privilege to work here. You may know the Queen, Mary Stuart, was attended by ladies who were all named Mary. She called them her 'Maries' because the Queen had had a French upbringing. Well, here we are some five hundred years later and the Queen is still attended by a Mary."

Paul and Amy smiled, but the group seemed unimpressed by this nugget of knowledge.

"Now what would the Queen of Scotland be doing in this pokey little border town? Oh, it's true! Our young people would tell you Jedburgh's the most boring place on earth. Unless that's where you live?"

Despite their disinclination to listen to any adult some of the group smiled.

"Any ideas what might've brought Mary here?"

Amy's eyes warned Paul not to offer an answer: a sure-fire way to bring down the wrath of the group and Miss Probert on their heads.

"No? Then let me enlighten you."

Mary MacDonald looked upon the closed faces of the teenagers.

What have we done to them that they close up whenever we try to share something?

For a moment she saw a flicker of sympathy in the eyes of the twins, boy and girl.

"Well, Mary Stuart and her escort came to Jedburgh to hold a Justice Ayres or Circuit Court, arriving in Jedburgh on the 9th October, 1566. Now how boring is that? On a scale of ten? Seven, eight, nine?"

"Eleven, miss," said Kevin and the girls laughed.

"It gets worse," the Custodian continued and emboldened, the boys groaned aloud.

"Mary was driven from her lodging in the Spread Eagle Hotel in High Street by a fire. This House, one of a series of fortified dwellings, was rented for her use."

Paul and Amy exchanged glances that Mary MacDonald picked up and grasped as a drowning custodian would a straw.

"You! The girl with auburn hair. What's your name?"

"Amy, miss," said Amy.

"You were listening to me."

Amy laughed and said, "It just seems odd. A fire when the Queen's in the Hotel? Wouldn't everyone be taking the greatest care?"

"Exactly," agreed Mary MacDonald, "Your first concern would be for her safety."

"Maybe somebody tried to murder her, miss?" suggested Paul, earning the eternal hatred of Miss Probert and the contempt of the History group.

"Now, you see," said the Custodian to the A Level History group, "this is where it stops being boring. Did someone try to murder the Queen of Scotland? To burn her to death in her bed? It was a pretty brutal, lawless time!"

The young faces displayed interest. Brutal was cool.

*

On the hillside above gloomy Hermitage Keep under scudding clouds and driving rain, Mary Stuart, shrouded in her cloak, calmed a restless horse, awaiting an answer from James Hepburn, Earl of Bothwell. Around her the horsemen of her company strived to shield the women from the worst of the storm, but no one dared suggest the Queen withdraw. Mary Stuart was the first to see movement from Hermitage. A horseman rode hard, struggling up the treacherous slope to the royal party.

The horseman, wind-whipped and rain-drowned, arrived to salute the Queen.

"Well? What is his answer?"

John Traquair, Captain of the Royal Bodyguard, shook his head and declared, "He will not let you pass, Majesty. He bids you welcome to Hermitage, but his intent is to seize and hold you hostage."

"There is no manner in which we can persuade him of his loyal duty?"

The Captain turned in his saddle to point to horsemen issuing from Hermitage Keep.

"If we linger he will take you by force of arms."

Mary turned her horse and the royal party pulled reins to bring their mounts about.

"Where to, Majesty?" asked Adam Blackwood, the Queen's Secretary.

"Back to the house at Jethart."

Blackwood and Traquair exchanged anxious glances.

The Queen put whip to her horse and the royal party fled for their lives.

*

The guard chamber of the House was in confusion. Exhausted horses steamed and stamped. Grooms struggled to clear harness and dry the horses. Drenched men-at-arms steamed at the great fire. The women had fled to the upper room to light a fresh fire for the Queen and lay out dry clothing. But the Queen remained with Blackwood and Traquair to watch the housemen bolt, bar and block the great door.

"This is not a house to withstand a purposed siege, Majesty" Traquair declared.

"It is the only refuge," Blackwood stated, "To press for Edinburgh they would have overtaken us."

"But we can defend the House?" Mary asked.

"To the death, Majesty," Traquair promised, "before they harm a hair of your head."

The pregnant Queen smiled upon her gallant knight.

"There speaks my gallant Traquair!"

"If they have cannon?" Blackwood suggested.

"They cannot move cannon in this mire," asserted Traquair, "If they had, we'd sally out and make short work of the engineers."

Adam Blackwood said, "A good man has been dispatched to Lord Darnley in Edinburgh, Majesty. We can most surely sustain a siege until your husband comes to our relief."

A marie came fluttering down the stairs into the guard chamber.

"There is movement on the far bank of the Jedwater, Majesty."

The trio moved to the arrow slit by the great door, but could see nothing through the driving rain and gathering darkness.

"They are here," Traquair decided, "but they won't come within bowshot."

"Majesty," said the marie timorously, "If you would ascend to your chamber?"

"Very well," the Queen agreed and followed the marie.

Calm was returning to the guard chamber. The House was secure. The horses were content, still steaming, but eating from nosebags. Grooms, housemen and men-at-arms sat about the fire, eating and drinking, embellishing the day's adventure.

"The siege has begun," sighed Blackwood.

"Then we will keep the House," agreed the stouthearted Traquair, "And rely on Lord Darnley for relief."

Something in Traquair's tone made Adam Blackwood laugh.

*

"You're waiting for me to tell you, yes or no," Mary MacDonald said, "But I'm not going to. You'll have to exercise your own noddles. But I'll tell you this."

She held her audience spellbound in the dim twilight of the guard chamber of the ancient House.

"Mary made a perilous ride through wild hill country from Jedburgh to Hermitage Castle in Liddesdale, where James Hepburn, Earl of Bothwell, was reported to lie wounded from a skirmish with border reivers. Who was this James Hepburn? Why did she ride to see him?"

She didn't expect an answer, but hid her surprise when Vickie exclaimed, "He was her lover, miss?"

"So she rode to Hermitage, fearful for her life? Through a terrible storm to the man she loved? Looking to Bothwell to help her?"

Mary MacDonald looked round on the young faces.

"Then why did she return to the House the same day? Losing a shoe in the morass on the way. Did he refuse her sanctuary because he was afraid? Fearful for his own safety?"

Gillian said, "That's what men do, miss," and nobody laughed.

"So," said the Custodian, "The story of Mary and the House has stopped being boring. It's now an unsolved mystery story."

"But what happened, miss?" said Alan, tentatively, "When she got back here."

"Mary fell sick and her condition became so desperate that her recovery was despaired of."

"Perhaps she was poisoned, miss?" Vickie suggested.

*

Following the group up the shadowed stairs, Paul almost bumped into a teenage girl on the mid-stairs landing dressed in Stuart costume.

"Sorry," said Paul, "Me clumsy oaf."

"Very authentic," said Amy, admiring the costume, "Do you work here? Or is it a project?"

The young woman seemed about to speak when Colin rushed up the stairs from below and walked through the girl in Stuart costume as if she weren't there: which seconds later she wasn't.

The twins were shocked and breathless.

Did that really happen?

I don't want to believe it did, but it did.

She was about to speak to us.

They stood in a shadowed silence.

Do you feel that?

Paul nodded.

It's like. It's like the house is crowded.

We're not the only people here. There's a whole, a whole other-world rubbing elbows with us.

Are you frightened?

Paul shook his head.

No. But there are people here who are frightened.

Something terrible is happening. Here in the House. Now!

Paul reached for Amy's hand.

Did you feel that? Somebody has just died. In the guard chamber.

They turned to go down the stairs when a familiar voice stopped them.

"Where do you think you're going?" Miss Probert demanded.

"Miss, we," Amy said and stopped.

"Perhaps you'd be so kind as to join the group?"

"Yes, miss."

"Don't think you fool me," Miss Probert asserted.

"No, miss."

What exactly is it that we're failing to fool her about?

Paul shrugged.

"Dumb insolence doesn't amuse me," said Miss Probert, "Report to detention tomorrow."

"Yes, miss," chorused the twins cheerfully.

*

"One of the most asked questions is?" suggested Mary MacDonald.

"When do we eat, miss?" Kevin asked.

Miss Probert frowned, but Mary MacDonald laughed with the group.

24

"You're right," she said, "I mustn't keep you much longer. I can hear tummies rumbling, but there is one question many visitors ask? Which is?"

An embarrassing silence greeted the Custodian's request. Miss Probert offered, encouragingly, "John? Gillian? What d'you think?"

Amy was surprised to find her hand rising, but Mary MacDonald nodded to her.

"Yes?"

"What did the Queen look like, miss?"

"You shall have the extra doughnut. What did the Queen look like? Well, we're very fortunate to have Mary's death mask."

To the puzzled faces she explained, "Sometimes with "celebrities" a cast was taken of the face at the time of death. Here is the Queen's death mask."

The group pressed forward to stare at the calm face of a long-dead Queen.

"She was perhaps as tall as you. What's your name?"

"Amy, miss," said Amy.

"And something of your colouring. Auburn tending to red."

"It's a beautiful face," said Amy and the girls murmured agreement. She could feel Paul was similarly disturbed by this sighting of the Queen.

"It seems so real," Amy commented, struggling to understand what she felt and why the face disturbed her so deeply.

*

There was a terrible silence in the hall of Fotheringhay following the hacking away of Mary's head and Amy heard the echo of that silence. She looked to Paul and saw him ashen-faced. When the Queen's head, stripped of wig and dignity, rolled across the floor that silence was rent apart by screams of terror that dissolved into endless weeping.

*

"But it is real," smiled Mary MacDonald, "As real as a death mask can be."

"I don't think I mean real, miss," Amy confessed, confused.

"Then what do you mean, Amy?"

"Close," said Paul, "She seems very close. Not distant."

"Yes," said Amy, "Close. That's what I mean."

"It seems to me you don't know what you mean," said Miss Probert.

To the Custodian, she added, "Amy is very much an attention-seeker. A very silly girl."

Mary MacDonald seemed about to object and then changed her mind.

Paul said, "That's not true, miss. I won't have you saying that about Amy. My sister is a very intelligent girl. If you can't share how moving this mask is, then I'm sorry for you!"

He immediately regretted his outburst.

"Her brother's much the same," retorted Miss Probert and some teenagers laughed.

"They always have to be different, miss," complained Gillian.

"I think," said Mary MacDonald, "it's time for lunch. I can definitely hear the tummy rumbles."

The A Level History group laughed and applauded.

"This afternoon feel free to write, draw, take photographs and if there are questions to answer you won't find me very far away. Now if you'll follow me."

As the group filed out of the House, blinking into the sunlight, the Custodian seemed to anticipate speaking to Amy and Paul. If this were so she was disappointed as Miss Probert bundled the twins past her without the opportunity to share a word.

THREE

Standing in the warm, insect-busy scented air of the garden Miss Probert declared, "Do not cause a nuisance in the shops. Remember you represent the school. I will expect you here at one thirty. No later."

When the group began to disperse she added, "But not you, Amy and Paul. You will confine yourselves to the garden."

Expecting dissent she was disappointed when Amy replied politely, "Thank you very much, miss," and Paul smiled his agreement happily.

*

Content to be in the flower-full garden, free of Miss Probert and the History group, Amy and Paul began to eat from their lunch boxes. Watching Paul wolf down his salami sandwiches Amy thought, How does Mum do it? Our lunch boxes are so different. She knows us too well. Even the treat. I love Aero and Paul would sell his soul for a Mars bar.

She laughed out loud and Paul said, "What's up?"

"Want to swap your Mars for my Aero?"

Paul shook his head, "No way!"

Into the pool of silence, broken only by birdsong, Paul said slowly, "I think it's like when we saw Granny Bowman. Remember? After she passed? They tried to persuade us we didn't. Told us we were mistaken. But we did see her."

"Granny Bowman came to tell us she was happy," Amy recalled, "We were not to be sad. But what's happening in the House is different."

"I wish Dad had believed us," Paul said, reflectively, "He was so unhappy."

Amy declared, "The girl we saw wanted to tell us something. Something important. Something frightening."

"Somebody died in the guard room," said Paul, "You felt it, didn't you?"

Amy nodded, "I believe she wanted our help."

Suddenly across the garden Paul saw the girl in Stuart dress again. "There she is!"

The girl, standing by the porch of the House, was urgently beckoning to them. The twins abandoned their lunch boxes and ran towards the marie.

As she ran Amy thought, A ghost in sunlight? Absolutely clear and solid?

"Three-dimensional," Paul said aloud, "Real as you or me!"

The distress in the maid's face gave way to fear. She called out to the teenagers words they couldn't hear, speaking as though through water. Suddenly she turned, face fearful, and ran back into the House.

"Wait!" cried Amy and Paul together, "We need to speak to you! Please!"

Then the marie was gone, as a shadow is lost in shadow. The twins stumbled and stopped, to stare at one another, bewildered.

Looking about them for a cause of her fear and flight the twins saw only a woman in sunglasses looking into the garden through the railings. She smiled at the teenagers: a very ordinary middle-aged woman. A boarding-house keeper, perhaps? Weekly Terms Agreeable.

"Don't stop your play for me," she said, smiling, "Isn't it just the queen of days?"

Amy agreed, saying, "Yes, a lovely day."

Turning away, Paul said, "She didn't see?"

Amy shook her head.

The woman called, "And where would you be from?"

"England," said Paul, and the woman smiling, said, "I thought so. That would be the place, right enough. England. Perhaps I'll see you again?"

"Not if I see you first," Paul said and Amy was abruptly embarrassed. It was unlike Paul to sound so hostile.

The woman smiled again and turned away, saying, "Enjoy your visit to the House."

Why did you say that? So rude!

There's something wrong about that woman.

That's silly. She was only being friendly.

Was she? Why would she ask where we came from?

That's the sort of thing people say. Where's the harm in saying Newcastle?

She didn't see the marie.

No.

But maybe the marie saw her?

Amy was suddenly cold and began to shiver. A cloud passed over the sun, casting the trees where the twins stood into deep shadow.

"But why would the marie run when she saw that woman?" Amy said aloud.

*

Cadet Timothy, black sack in hand, rapped on the open door of D.I. Harold Starling's office. The Inspector was at his desk, biro in hand, scrutinising a statement.

"Yes?"

"Can I get your rubbish, sir?"

"Be quick about it."

The cadet tipped the bin into his sack, shaking it to persuade the paper waste to co-operate. A solid object thumped into the sack. Timothy reached into his sack and pulled out a videotape case he recognised. He hesitated to speak to the Inspector.

"What's your name?"

"Cadet Timothy, sir."

"You know all paper has to be shredded before it's binned?"

"Yes, sir. I've been checked out on the shredder, sir."

Plucking up courage he asked, "The tape, sir?"

"What tape?"

D.I. Starling stared at the videotape case as if he'd never seen it before.

"Well, you can't put that through the shredder."

"No, sir."

"Pull out the tape, cut it up, stamp on the case. Break it as you did your Thomas the Tank Engine tapes."

"I never had any Thomas the Tank Engine videos, sir."

"Just smash it."

"Yes, sir. Thank you, sir."

The cadet exited the D.I.'s office smartly and moved on to the next waste bin.

*

Reluctantly leaving the delights of Jedburgh High Street the group returned, in ones and twos, to join Miss Probert and the twins for the afternoon session.

Well, at least she can't pick on us for being late, thought Paul, which made Amy laugh, and Miss Probert to glare at their innocent faces. Gillian brought Miss Probert a present of a packet of Jedburgh Jellies.

*

Working quietly in a corner of the upper room Amy drew the Stuart maid she and Paul saw in the garden.

"May I see?"

Looking up, Amy found Mary MacDonald smiling at her.

"It's not very good, miss," she said, surrendering her sketchpad.

She was surprised when the Custodian said, "Good heavens!" and vanished saying, "I'll be back in a moment!"

This unexpected attention caught the eye of Miss Probert.

"Now what have you done, Amy?"

"Nothing, miss," she protested, aware of Paul making notes at the case containing the death mask, pleading, *Please don't interfere, Paul. Just let her rave on!*

"Can't be nothing when you've obviously upset Miss MacDonald."

"I didn't do anything, miss."

"You must've done something."

"She wanted to look at my drawing. Then she just went off."

"Then you should apologise."

"For what, miss?"

Mary MacDonald returned carrying Amy's sketchpad and a small, framed picture.

"I think you should see this, Miss Probert."

The teacher said, "I've spoken to Amy and she's ready to apologise."

Amy cast a despairing glance at Paul; *We're living in an insane asylum!*

"I can't imagine why," said Mary MacDonald, holding up the sketchpad and the framed picture.

"Quite remarkable! This is a picture of Mary Seton, one of the Queen's maries. This is Amy's drawing. A splendid likeness, is it not?"

Amy was startled at the similarity between her drawing and the picture of the Marie. She sensed Paul beside her.

At least now we know her name. Mary Seton.

"A good copy," admitted Miss Probert grudgingly, "but anyone can copy someone else's work."

Amy said, surprised, "I've never seen that picture before."

Mary MacDonald regarded Amy thoughtfully.

"If I'd copied the picture I would say so, miss," Amy explained, "That's the girl we saw when," and then caught herself.

The Custodian said, "This House sometimes has a remarkable effect upon visitors. Well done, Amy! Now you know who she is."

"A very fanciful young woman," said Miss Probert.

"She always has to be so mysterious, miss," said Gillian, forever in harmony with the teacher.

"Perhaps she is," commented Mary MacDonald, "Mysterious, that is."

*

The Custodian set the burglar alarm in the inner porch and stepped out to join the school party, smiling.

"Yes, we do have burglar alarms. In the sixteenth century they would have employed geese and mastiffs."

She displayed a heavy antique key and said, "Who would like to lock the door?" and then ignored every plea to present the key to a surprised Amy.

"We'll turn it together, shall we?"

They turned their backs on the disappointed group. Mary MacDonald said quietly to Amy, "Be careful, my dear, won't you? You're very special."

Amy was too surprised to reply.

From the lane the coach signalled its arrival.

"Thank you all for coming," said the Custodian, "You've been a very good group. Do come and see us again soon."

These last words were directed with a certain emphasis to Amy and Paul. The group, calling their thanks, scattered for the coach.

Mary MacDonald said to Miss Probert, "It's been an especial pleasure meeting you, my dear. Let's hope we never meet again. Goodbye."

Which left Miss Probert somewhat puzzled and disturbed.

*

When the coach pulled away Amy saw Mary Seton again at an upper window. Her face was pleading and fearful. Amy nudged her brother who nodded, but when she opened her mouth to tell Miss Probert, Paul whispered, "What's the point? They have eyes and see not."

The key is in the lock
And the door opens
The secrets of the abyss to reveal.

They regarded one another anxiously.

"Someone," said Paul, "is putting words in our mouth," echoed Amy.

"I'm frightened, Paul," whispered Amy.

"Forget it," said her brother, "We'll be home in an hour."

"You two are always whispering," said Melanie, "It's disgusting! They have a word for what you are."

To which Paul answered, "And for you too, Mel. One starting with bee."

But Amy knew she would not forget what had happened at the Queen's House.

*

On the long winding road to Carter Bar the coach collected a string of cars unable to pass as a convoy of military vehicles descended into Scotland. The coach driver dropped a gear as the last of the convoy swept past and cars began to overtake until there was only a single car following the coach. This driver made no attempt to pass. The coach driver signalled the road ahead was clear of traffic and dropped a further gear, but the driver behind made no attempt to overtake. The coach driver studied the following vehicle and smiled to himself. The car was a venerable Morris Traveller.

How many of them are still on the road? the coach driver wondered and lost interest.

The coach reached the crest and despite the teenagers' pleas to stop began the long descent into England. The Morris Traveller didn't stop at the border either, but continued to follow the coach down the winding road into Northumberland.

If the driver of the old Morris had been asked his name, and answered truthfully, which is unlikely, he would have pronounced James Hepburn, and smiled his crooked smile: a handsome man with unruly hair and the face of a dark angel. His smaller companion, his head below seat level, would have scowled and refused to answer. His name was Cymian and those who knew him would shiver at his name.

*

As Paul and Amy walked along Wellington Terrace, Gosforth, the old Morris Traveller parked clumsily behind them, riding the kerb. As Paul put his key into the lock of number thirty-nine the driver of the Morris Traveller was pulling on the handbrake to stall the engine. When Paul and Amy stepped into the entrance hall of thirty-nine and

33

Paul called out, "We're home, Mum! Kill the fatted calf!" the driver and his companion were climbing out of the Morris Traveller.

The children's mother came bustling to the door, coat unbuttoned, briefcase in one hand and sheet from a note pad in the other.

"Too late," cried Joyce Bowman, "You'll have to kill the fatted calf yourselves. I've written you a note. Don't stay up too late!"

She kissed them both as she exited.

"Did you have a good day?"

Half way to the car Joyce Bowman turned to call to the teenagers standing in the doorway, "I nearly forgot! Your father would like you to stay with him for the half-term. Ring him if you want to go. I have to fly. Find yourself something to eat. Bye!"

The car door slammed, the engine started and Joyce Bowman drove away, leaving Amy's "What time'll you be back?" hanging in the wind.

"We haven't got a mother," said Paul, "She's a Kansas twister."

Paul closed the front door on the world and Amy read from the note.

"Sorry. Been asked to cover for Carole. Whoever Carole is. Hear about Jedburgh tomorrow. Love you both. Mum."

Amy headed for the kitchen.

"You ring Dad. I'll raid the freezer."

She opened the freezer, thinking, *Mum worries me. She doesn't take the Connellys seriously. Thoroughly nasty people. It wasn't Mum's fault Lisa Connelly and her baby died. But the Connellys don't see it like that.*

Paul came into the kitchen, saying, "No good worrying about Mum. Mum is Mum."

"What did Dad say?"

"He wasn't there."

"As ever, like Macavity," Amy said, "It's all Siberian mammoth flesh in here. Chinese takeaway?"

"Are you offering?"

Amy sighed, "I suppose so. What do you do with your money, Paul?"

He grinned and said, "I'm saving up for my old age."

"What old age? You won't last that long."

*

The teenagers went out into the twilight of Wellington Terrace, talking of cabbages and kings and why the sea is boiling hot and whether pigs have wings. As they crossed the road a car approached and they stood together waiting for the car to pass.

Then as if in a dream Amy saw from the corner of her eye what was not possible in a rational universe. From the shadow of the hedge stepped a dwarfish figure, clad in mail shirt and leg wrappings, an iron cap on his head. This apparition had a crossbow in his hand. All this, Amy, unbelieving, saw clearly and turned to Paul who watched the approaching car.

"Paul!" she cried, "Look at that!"

The dwarf fired his bolt at the approaching car. The bolt ricocheted from the shattered windscreen, which blinded the driver who instinctively pulled away.

Amy saw the car looming at them even as Paul tried desperately to push her aside. The car struck the teenagers with an indescribable fleshy sound, killing Paul instantly. Amy had a glimpse of the blind windscreen before the car caught her, throwing her across the road. The car careered across the farther pavement into a garden wall. Beyond the crash and trickle of fallen bricks the silence began.

Lying in the roadway, Amy, fighting for consciousness, heard approaching feet. The boots stopped and she stared up disbelievingly into the face of the dwarf looking down at her.

"Help me," she whispered, "Please!"

The wolfish face smiled down at her. She heard a car approach and stop. Amy, the storm of pain arising, consciousness fading, saw the opening door. She glimpsed cowboy boots as the driver reached over to open the door. The dwarf scrambled into the car. Through the gathering mist Amy glimpsed the Morris Traveller drive away. Then darkness overwhelmed her and though she cried out for Paul. There was no answer.

The street was silent until a man and woman ran out from a gateway. Then the voices began.

FOUR

The double doors crashed open as the ambulance trolley forced its way through into the evening clamour of Casualty. Amy glimpsed the changing pattern of ceiling lights as doctor and nurses bent over her: machine gun bursts of professional shorthand bombarded her ears.

Then suddenly she was back in the garden at the Jethart House under the wheeling shadow of pigeons, shading her eyes to follow their flight to where the Stuart maid, eyes wide with fear, beckoned her urgently. Amy ran to sit with her and Mary Seton began to speak, but Amy couldn't hear what the marie said for the growing buzz of intruding voices.

Amy struggled to sit up on the A&E trolley, crying, "Please, oh, please, be quiet! I can't hear what she's saying."

The casualty nurse gently, but firmly restrained the road accident victim.

"Shush, lie down, darling, lie down, there's a good girl!"

"I can't hear what she's saying!"

"Don't worry, darling! Everything's going to be alright!"

"It's the Queen! She's in deadly danger! I know she is!"

Doctor and nurse looked at one another. The young doctor tried to suppress a grin and failed. The nurse pressed the plunger of the hypodermic and darkness descended on Amy.

*

When the pigeon fluttered against the window Joyce Bowman awoke with a guilty start. She discovered herself lying on Paul's bed. She had fallen asleep. Fallen asleep! The flames of guilt roared. How could I! Paul's scent on the bedclothes brought her to tears again and she struggled to contain her grief. She lay looking at the ceiling, at the specks of Blutak and the odd thread from which had hung Paul's aerial armada until he had suddenly grown up when his father left home.

Abandoned us, Joyce thought, *not left home. My son tore down and destroyed the aeroplanes father and son had spent so much happy time constructing.*

From within the plastic carapace of Paul's alarm clock Mickey Mouse nodded at her sympathetically.

Why don't you go downstairs, Joyce, and have something to eat? Mickey suggested, *You haven't eaten since.*

"I'm not hungry," Joyce said aloud.

You need to be strong for Amy.

Joyce said aloud, "I'm alright. I'll get something later," but she knew she was lying. She would never be all right again.

Amy! she thought, *I must get myself moving.*

*

Mercifully the coma had been short-lived. On the fourth morning a sudden movement of Amy's hand had awakened her mother dozing in the bedside chair.

Amy mumbled, "I had this dream, Mum," but her mother was pressing the alarm for the nurse and wasn't listening.

"Where's Paul?" said Amy.

"Lie still, darling and don't talk," Joyce advised.

"I want to see Paul," Amy insisted.

Her mother complained, "Where is that nurse?"

"I can't hear him," said Amy.

"Hear who?" her mother asked.

"Paul," Amy said, "I can't hear him. He's not there."

A doctor and two nurses arrived and Joyce Bowman stood aside.

*

Detective Constable Susan Duffy was about to leave the station yard when D.C. Malpas appeared in front of the car. Susan wound down the window.

She declared, "I am not going to the prom with you. Don't ask me again."

D.C. Malpas, an older detective, was the only man on the squad she liked.

Malpas grinned and said, "Mitchell wants to see you."

"Now?"

"Now!"

Susan parked the car and went to find the Detective Sergeant. She found him where he could always be found; in the canteen. The young detective sat down at his table and watched him load half a steak and kidney pie into his cavernous mouth. She waited patiently while he masticated the mouthful and asked, "What did you want to see me about, Sarge? I'm on my way to baby-sit Doctor Bowman. I'm supposed to be there for two."

She checked her watch while the sergeant ingested the remainder of the pie and chewed it thoroughly before swallowing. She waited while he washed it down with half a mug of tea.

"I really should be moving, Sarge."

"That's what I wanted to see you about," Mitchell said, clearing a fragment of steak from between his front teeth, inspecting his prize and popping it back into his mouth.

"Yes?"

"You've been rubbed. Griffiths is going to take it."

Susan struggled to hide her feelings. Mitchell cleaned up the peas with a glue of mashed potato and refilled his mouth. Susan fought not to say what she was thinking.

She contrived to say, "Who says?"

"The D.I."

"Why?"

"The hospital put in a request for security. There may be a connection with the Connollys. Her son died in an R.T.A. So Starling wants to humour them."

Susan said, "I could humour her. I'm good at humouring people."

"The Connollys," said the sergeant, wiping his mouth on a paper serviette and reaching for his dessert of spotted dick and custard, "aren't averse to using a shooter."

Susan declared, "I've faced a man with a gun in his hand."

D.S. Mitchell shrugged without declaring his private opinion that the muppet gave up because he wouldn't shoot a woman.

"The D.I. wants a man on it. You can do the schools."

Susan insisted, "I've tackled a maniac with a knife."

"Why don't you have a chat with our Harold?" Mitchell said and smiled.

"A waste of time," Susan declared, "And a waste of space."

She rose from her chair, saying, "By the way you've got gravy on your tie," leaving the fat man peering down at his spotless tie.

*

As her feet touched the floor someone rang the front door bell.

"Sugar and tapioca!" Joyce cried and looked round in vain for shoes or slippers. The bell rang insistently and Joyce went downstairs in her stockinged feet.

If it's the Mormons, it's gonna be a day they won't forget.

She opened the front door.

"Oh, it's you," she said, "What d'y'want?"

Joyce's ex-husband, Derek Bowman, said, "Wha'd'y'think I want? Our son's been murdered."

Joyce allowed him into the hallway. He was as always, crumpled, hair receding fast, still overweight, but the same, impish mischievous face; a born salesman.

But never again, Derek, will you sweet-talk me.

"You took your time."

"Long way from Berlin."

"You walked?"

Joyce surveyed the peaceful world of Wellington Terrace.

"Is she with you? Dearest Melissa? Love of your life?"

"Is that your toy boy? Out there? In the car? Giving me funny looks."

He grinned at her, the same old seductive grin.

You've never grown up and you never will.

From the hallway the young detective constable, David Griffiths, was visible in the unmarked car at the kerb.

"Don't be so stupid! He's a policeman."

"At least they're doing that much," Derek Bowman agreed, "Because it's not finished yet."

"What isn't?"

"The Connollys killed my son. It'll be you or Amy next."

Joyce struggled to contain her emotions.

"Paul's death," she said slowly, determined not to weep, "was an accident. A tragedy. But not murder."

"It wasn't an accident!" Derek Bowman retorted angrily, "It was murder!"

"I don't believe that," Joyce cried, "I won't believe that!"

"These people aren't rational. They blame you for what happened."

"I wasn't even in the hospital."

"You were the consultant."

"Lisa Connolly was a meth addict. The baby didn't stand a chance. Born into addiction. It was all explained to them. The risks. But they weren't listening."

"They've threatened to kill you," said Derek Bowman, "Our son's dead. Don't you see any connection?"

Joyce said, feebly, "I don't want to hear this."

Derek insisted, "The Connollys are gangsters. They mean what they say."

"Nobody takes those people seriously," said Joyce.

"They take you seriously enough to kill our son."

"Paul's death was a tragic accident."

Derek sighed heavily.

"I read about Councillor Gibson opposing planning permission for the Connollys entertainment complex, a.k.a casino. Surprise, surprise, his house burned down."

They stood in an angry silence in the hallway.

"Joyce, please, listen to me," said Derek Bowman, "Paul's death wasn't an accident. One of those nutters killed our son. He would've killed Amy too."

"It was an accident," Joyce persisted.

"Haven't you read the driver's statement?"

"Yes."

"He says a missile was thrown at his car windscreen. Deliberately to blind him.

He knows it wasn't an accident. And the plod outside knows it was murder."

"I don't want you in my house," Joyce said, "Please leave."

"All I'm asking," Derek Bowman pleaded, "is for you to take care. Think about resigning from the hospital. Let it all calm down. Take the warning."

Joyce Bowman said, "Are you leaving? Or do I ask the policeman to move you?"

Her ex-husband moved to depart, but gestured towards the car.

"How long is Plod gonna hang about?"

"I don't know."

"Well, he won't stay forever."

"I didn't ask for him."

"When he goes. What then?"

Joyce had no answer.

Derek Bowman turned to go, descending the steps to the path.

"I'm here if you need me. At the Marriott."

"We don't need you."

She watched him walk to the gate, anger subsiding, but he didn't look back. Derek Bowman spoke to the young detective in the car and walked away.

Joyce closed the front door and went to ascend the stairs. On a sudden impulse she sat on a lower step and began to weep.

The front door bell rang.

Is there no peace?

Joyce rose, wiped her eyes, determined to ignore the summons, when she heard the voice of the young detective call from outside.

"Doctor Bowman?"

Obediently, she went to open the door.

"Yes?"

David Griffiths enquired, "I thought you might need some company?"

"Then you thought wrong."

Joyce turned to ascend the stairs.

"You can't spend the rest of your life sitting on Paul's bed."

As soon as the words left his lips David Griffiths regretted speaking.

Without turning her head Joyce snapped, "It's still my house. I can do what I want."

"There's Amy to consider."

Joyce turned to look at the young man.

"Sorry I spoke," he said, "But it's true."

"What exactly are your orders, Detective Constable Griffiths?"

"See you come to no harm, Doctor Bowman."

"Does that include telling me what to do?"

The detective almost smiled.

"Can't see anyone ever telling you what to do, doctor. But I do have some experience of tragic circumstances such as this."

"Oh," Joyce said, softening, mollified.

"My mother. After my father was killed. A difficult time."

"He was a police officer?" Joyce asked although intuitively she knew the answer.

"Cup of tea, doctor?" the detective asked and Joyce followed him towards the kitchen.

*

The forest canopy was midnight dark and rain-laden, with a flicker of stars above.

Beyond the fleeting clouds the gibbous moon hung heavy. Every innocent shade became shapeless while the shapeless dark assumed menacing form. Amy ran through the trees, breath heaving, lungs wheezing, afraid for her life. Behind she heard the clamour of pursuit: the voices of men, the tongues of dogs. Over the rise, astride a lathered horse, rode the man with the face of a dark angel. Men-at-arms ran at his stirrups. Why she was running and from whom Amy did not understand, but she knew survival depended on the sureness of her feet. Amy ran towards the great oak whose branches straddled the path. Could she find sanctuary if she climbed unseen?

As she panted towards the oak a dwarf she knew, but did not know, dropped from a branch and stood, grinning in her path. Amy stopped, frozen with fear.

The dwarf bowed and said, "Ill-met, milady! Did thee think to outwit Cymian?"

Amy cried, "Why are you doing this? What have I ever done to you?"

The dwarf raised the cross bow and sighted on her breast.

"Not what, but what yet you may do, milady," the dwarf replied and his finger closed upon the trigger. The bolt flew true to its aim.

*

Evening is the best of times in any hospital. The battles of the day have been fought, won or lost. Visitors came to and departed from almost every bed. The ward buzzed as a contented hive. Amy lay sleeping in a corner bed, her arm tethered by an umbilical drip to a hanging bag; the crystal fluid reflected the early evening light. The nurse at her bedside, marking the chart, looked up and smiled at Amy's parents.

Derek Bowman asked, "How's she doing?"

The nurse said, "Amy's doing well. As you know she's been very lucky."

Joyce Bowman smiled wryly.

"As I understand it," said the nurse, "her brother threw her out of the way of the car. He saved her life."

And died for her, thought Joyce*, my brave, brave boy.*

Without surprise she found herself holding her ex-husband's hand very tightly.

The nurse said to Amy's father, "Amy has two broken ribs. Fracture of the humerus. And she smacked her head on the concrete. Nasty!"

"But the coma?" said Derek Bowman.

"When the brain comes into violent contact with a rock or a hard place it will shut down to protect itself. Sometimes the trauma is extreme. Amy has been very fortunate."

Joyce and Derek, mother and father, sat on opposite sides of the bed: together and yet apart. As she sat down Joyce caught the eye of the old woman in the next bed and said, "Good evening! Please excuse my back, won't you?"

The old woman, bright-eyed, sparrow-small, returned the smile, but raised a hand to her throat indicating she had no voice.

"Oh, I'm sorry!" said Joyce.

Though why I'm apologising I don't know.

The old woman waved away her concern and gestured towards Amy.

"Yes," Joyce agreed, "My daughter. Amy. Road accident."

I'm talking pidgin English as if she were mentally disadvantaged!

She felt impelled to introduce Derek who smiled across at the old woman as she said, "My husband. Amy's father."

She could have bitten off her tongue, but it was too late to take back the words. *What the fiddle and bow is wrong with me?*

Derek smiled at Joyce and said to the old woman, "Amy's been very lucky. It could've been much worse."

Why on earth did I say that? My husband? He's not my husband. If this is the menopause I will shoot myself!

She glared at Derek who was holding Amy's hand in his bear paws, kissing her fingertips.

If you think for one minute, Derek Bowman, that I would.

Derek looked up and said, "What?" and Amy woke up.

Drowsy Amy said, "Hi, Mum! You haven't brought more grapes, have you?"

Joyce let the plastic sack of grapes slide back into the carrier bag.

"We're up to our ears in grapes! If we ate them all there'd be twice the queue for the loo."

Then she stopped, suddenly aware someone sat at the other side of the bed and gaped at her father.

"Dad? Dad! Is it you? It is you! Not the dope, is it?"

Derek Bowman laughed and said, "No, it's your old Dad, the only dope round here."

"What're you doing here?"

"Just passing on my way to the White House and thought I'd look in."

Amy laughed aloud, a sound of pure joy, and winced.

That's the first time she's laughed since, thought Joyce, *instantly guilty, and it's deceitful Derek made her laugh.*

"No, you weren't! But you're supposed to be in Berlin! What're you doing here?"

Her father swallowed her hands in his and said, "Where else would I be? I came to see you, muppet. Soon as I heard."

Amy was silent and Joyce thought, *If he makes her cry I'll kick his bum.* She felt cheated and guilty. *Why guilty? I might as well be invisible here!*

Joyce was oddly grateful for the interruption when a shadow fell across the bed. A porter with a trolley had stopped to refresh Amy's water jug. Doctor Bowman pushed her chair aside to allow a handsome man with unruly hair and the face, someone once remarked, of a dark angel, to retrieve and return the replenished water jug. He thanked her politely and asked Amy, "Would you wish me to pour you a glass of water?"

Amy shook her head, barely glancing into his face, too concerned with the presence of her father to notice any resemblance to a certain picture in the Jethart House; a portrait of James Hepburn, Earl Bothwell.

When the bell rang for the end of visiting time Joyce struggled with overwhelming self-pity. Amy had given all her attention to her estranged father. When they left Joyce was barely offered a word whilst Amy hugged Derek despite her mother's protests. *I might as well not be here.*

When they parted company in the car park Joyce was secretly pleased to discover Derek's parking ticket had fallen to the floor and he had been awarded a penalty notice.

"Oh, that's outrageous!" she sympathised falsely, "If I were you I'd fight it all the way to Brussels." *And they'll double the penalty. And hopefully hang you!*

As her car lights swung away, Derek Bowman was illuminated in argument with a parking warden and Joyce laughed out loud. She was immediately ashamed of her behaviour.

I'm turning into a very nasty person, she thought, *my son is dead. My daughter is in hospital and I'm jealous of her love for her father. What a despicable creature you are, Joyce! But did you see his face when he saw the ticket?*

45

Doctor Bowman turned into a side street, parked and turned off lights and engine. She wept until there were no more tears to shed. Detective Constable David Griffiths in the car parked behind her, had the good sense not to interfere.

*

When her parents departed, Amy lay awake as the ward settled down to watch television, read, chat and sleep.

Something is wrong. I can't hear Paul. P'rhaps it's the drugs? Why hasn't he been to see me? The black thought crept into her head. *Has he been hurt? And no one wants to tell me. But if he were somewhere in the hospital, I would know. He would talk to me. Unless something has happened to me. My head. I hurt my head. I hurt my head very badly. Have I gone deaf?*

She was suddenly afraid she would never hear Paul again.

FIVE

Amy became aware that the Drugs Round cabinet had arrived at the foot of her bed. A nurse she didn't know said brightly, "Amy Bowman?" Amy nodded agreement and the nurse came to check her wristband. As she was preparing her medication Amy asked, "Do these drugs affect people's heads?"

"In what way?" the nurse asked, pouring water and bringing medication to Amy.

"Make their brain work different?"

Amy swallowed the tablets and returned the little cup and glass.

The nurse checked Amy's chart.

"Could do, I suppose. But only temporary. Pain control is serious stuff. But I wouldn't worry about it. It'll pass."

The nurse moved on to the next patient and Amy lay down, somewhat mollified, but still uneasy.

A young woman came into the ward and spoke to the nurse who pointed out Amy's bed. Amy watched her approach. *I shouldn't have spoken to the nurse. Now they think I'm loopy.*

The young woman, red hair and freckles, clutching a bulging box file, smiled at Amy and said, "Hello, Amy! I'm Gabrielle."

Amy said, "I didn't mean it about my brain not working."

Gabrielle appeared puzzled and said, "That's good to hear. You don't know me, but I work as a teacher in the hospital."

She stopped, seeing from Amy's face that perhaps she wasn't too fond of teachers.

"I'm not going to bother you because you're not going to be here very long. But students your age do worry about A Levels."

"I'm not worrying about A Levels," Amy said, "The last thing I'd worry about is exams."

Gabrielle smiled and said, "Good! Don't. I can see you're a sensible girl. So I'll see you, Amy, only if you start to worry the nurses."

The teacher turned to go, but Amy said, "Don't go. Please."

Gabrielle turned back to the bed.

"Yes?"

"What really happened to the Queen?"

"Which Queen?"

"Mary, Queen of Scots."

Amy indicated Paul's copy of Antonia Fraser's Mary Queen of Scots lying on her locker top; the first thing she had demanded her mother bring.

Gabrielle hesitated, then smiled and said, "After what you've been through, you're supposed to say. . . Where am I? Not ask questions about your history project."

Amy pleaded, "Please? What happened to her?"

"She was imprisoned by Elizabeth I and executed at Fotheringhay."

"No," Amy insisted, "What happened to her at Jethart?"

Gabrielle hesitated and then said, "What do you know about Jethart?"

Amy was surprised she knew the archaic form of Jedburgh.

Amy explained, "On the ninth of October, fifteen sixty-six, Mary and her escort arrived in Jethart to hold a Circuit Court. She rode to the Hermitage to see Bothwell and came back the same day in distress. Then what happened to her?"

Gabrielle stood silent looking at the girl in the bed. *She has eyes of two different colours,* thought Amy, *how odd! One gray, one blue!*

Amy said, "I know something happened. Something terribly important for Mary. I need to know the truth."

"The truth isn't always in the books," said Gabrielle, "Sometimes it's hidden or destroyed."

"It may already be too late," said Amy, "But I want to know. I need to know."

It may already be too late? What'm I saying? Five hundred years ago may be too late? This woman must think I'm out of my mind.

"I know who you are," Gabrielle said, "You are the Gemini."

48

Amy was taken by surprise. The teacher moved closer to her, closing the screen.

Amy could smell her fragrance; the sweetness of the Jethart House garden. Every sound, every whisper of human voice and television ceased in the ward.

Amy faltered, "Don't know what you mean."

"Beware the man Bothwell," said Gabrielle, "A very dangerous man."

Amy struggled to understand.

"Mary's husband? Earl Bothwell? You said is! But he's been."

Amy was overcome by a sudden flush of anger.

"Why do you talk in riddles? Why doesn't anyone ever speak the simple truth?"

I'm in hospital. Is this really happening? Am I hallucinating? If I can form the word hallucinating does that mean I am or I am not?

The nurse turned in her chair at the voice raised in anger.

"Hallucinating," said Amy aloud and nothing changed.

Gabrielle whispered, "Because the truth isn't born yet. I pray you and your brother will find the truth."

"My brother is dead," said Amy, "Didn't you know that? He's dead. Knocked down by a car and killed."

The nurse stood up and came towards the corner bed.

"Nurse is coming to turn me out. Fear not. We will watch out for you."

"You and whose army?" Amy asked, amused.

The nurse arrived at the corner bed and opened the screen.

"I'm just going, Good night, Amy. Perhaps I'll see you tomorrow?"

The nurse stood by Amy's bed and watched Gabrielle leave the ward.

"What were you two arguing about?"

"Nothing."

"A noisy nothing," said the nurse, losing interest.

"You know what teachers are like," Amy said. "Always want the last word."

The nurse laughed and asked, "But you're going to settle down now? You're not going to make trouble for me, are you?"

"I wouldn't dare," said Amy and the nurse laughed.

She folded back the screens and returned to her desk. Amy mouthed goodnight at the old woman in the next bed who smiled in return and settled down to sleep. The old woman lay watching the girl until her own eyelids flickered and sleep overtook her.

*

Gabrielle was fumbling for her key in the car park when a figure materialised behind her and broke her neck. She died without a whimper. Cymian dragged the corpse to the Morris Traveller and pushed it into the rear. After a kangaroo start, Bothwell drove the car badly to the river where the pair borrowed a dinghy.

Cymian rowed to the shadow of the Redheugh Bridge where none kept watch. Bothwell slipped Gabrielle's corpse into the Tyne, her jacket and trousers packed with stones to delay her discovery. On the roof of the Nissan in the hospital car park the catch on the overburdened box file finally parted. The wind began to decorate the car park with sheets of A4.

*

Midnight in the hospital ward was an oasis of false calm. A woman snored, woke and snored again. A girl's voice called from the depths of sleep. Amy's neighbour, the old woman, awoke from dreams of childhood in a Northumbrian farmhouse and lay listening to the night sounds. On Amy's locker lay the book, Mary Queen of Scots. The ward door flapped open and closed. Draught stirred the pages to lie open to the portrait of James Hepburn, Earl of Bothwell.

The Sister and the night nurse, Nina Paice, walked the ward together to check the patients. Satisfied, the Sister left the young nurse with a brief word of praise. Nina walked the ward again and adjusted Amy's drip. She examined the portrait on the open page, closed the book with a tissue to keep Amy's place and tidied up the locker top. Nina returned to the desk and completed the night-book. Studying for an exam, she opened her study-file and became absorbed. Silence reigned on the ward; all battles yet to be fought postponed until dawn.

The ward door opened and wagged shut. Nina turned her head to see a porter emerge from the gloom bearing two cups of coffee. She smiled at him, happy to have his company; an attractive man bearing gifts.

"Do I know you?"

He smiled at her, offering the coffee, which she accepted gratefully.

"I think not."

"I feel I've seen you somewhere?"

For a moment the image flickered and faded as the turning of the pages of a book.

"You're new?" Nina guessed.

The porter smiled and her pulse quickened.

"How is the drink?"

"Fine," said the nurse, studying the porter.

A little harsh? Real coffee? This didn't come from the machine. They must have everything in that porters' room!

The porter stood sipping and the nurse cuddled her cup, drinking deep, glad of the company. *And he brought me coffee! Why me? He fancies me? Midnight romance? Ooh, lucky me!*

"Where are you from?" the nurse asked, smiling, hesitating, "You're not English, are you?"

The porter laughed to say, "God's blood, never English!"

Nina meant to ask him about the odd exclamation he used, but her mouth and throat were tingling; a burning sensation spread rapidly from throat to stomach.

She felt burning hot and freezing cold; her legs began to twitch uncontrollably. Her fingers started to curl with cramp. Nina started to say, "What's in this," but her throat closed.

"Wolfsbane," said the porter, "A sure remedy for all ills."

Nina tried to scream as her eyesight faded; her last image that of the porter smiling, toasting her with his coffee cup. The porter took the cup from her failing hand. Nina Paice struggled to stand up, lost control of her bladder, and died. James Hepburn caught her corpse to prop it up in the chair, head flopping to one side, vacant eyes staring at study tasks that would never now be completed.

James Hepburn crossed the ward to Amy's bed. He stood looking down at her for a moment. From his overall pocket he took out a syringe. The slight noise, metal upon metal, caused the old woman in the next bed to open an eye. She lay watching the porter, but unable to speak.

Surprised at what the man was doing, the old woman exclaimed silently, but then did not move, did not dare to move. Eyes wide open, she watched horrified as the porter injected Amy's drip bag. A purple curl drifted in the fluid, dispersing, sinking towards the capillary tube.

As the porter turned away from the bed the old woman shut her eyes. James Hepburn crossed to the night-desk and picked up the coffee cups. He regarded the corpse of the nurse for a long moment and then he was gone, the ward door wagging shut behind him.

The old woman struggled to call out and failed. Frustrated, she fought to bring her feet over the bed edge aware of the poison sinking slowly in the drip-bag. With a heart-searing effort the old woman forced herself to her feet. For a moment she remained upright. Then her feeble legs buckled and she fell. Falling she brought down the stand, tearing the needle from Amy's arm. The old woman was dead before her head hit the floor.

*

Detective Constable David Griffiths awoke with a sudden sense of alarm. Beside him, his wife Isobel mumbled her protest and turned away. The illuminated dial read three twenty four. David lay awake, staring into the darkness. As his eyelids began to droop, somewhere in the house a door opened and closed.

Trying not to arouse Isobel, David slowly freed himself from the bedclothes and stood up. He tiptoed to the bedroom door and eased it open. The nightlight on the landing burned clearly. He closed the bedroom door behind him and silently opened Jack's door. The boy lay sleeping soundly. Buzz Lightyear stood sentinel on his pillow. No harm will come to your son on my watch, Buzz assured the anxious father. From here to infinity as long as the batteries last. David closed the door and stood listening on the landing.

Downstairs in the kitchen the refrigerator began to sing. David walked across the landing to Caroline's room and opened her door. He stood at the cot looking down on his daughter surrounded by a chorus of teddies. The toddler was sleeping peacefully, thumb in her mouth as ever. As her father bent to ease the thumb from her lips Caroline stirred and David retreated to the door, satisfied all was well.

David stood on the landing, listening to the night. In the road a car started up noisily and with a clashing of gears, drove away revving unnecessarily. *You're lucky I'm not out there, my friend,* thought David, *I'd stop and breath test you.* Outside the bedroom door, he hesitated and decided to check downstairs.

In the kitchen he filled a glass with milk and stood gazing out on the silent garden feeling guilty at how little he did to help and how much Isobel did out there. At her birthday barbeque he'd accepted compliments on how well the garden looked, aware of his wife's mocking smile.

On the front door the chain was in place. The deadlock was dead-locked. The kitchen door was locked and bolted. Returning to the stairs, he glanced into the living room. On the coffee table stood two tumblers and the brandy bottle Isobel's father had brought as a present for his son-in-law who didn't drink. To avoid it being wasted, Isobel's father had generously offered to drink it. The old man drank half the bottle on Christmas Day, but Isobel refused to allow her father to take the bottle with him on the drive home. Despite his protests about possible medical emergencies.

David picked up a tumbler. The stink of brandy filled his nostrils. The second too had been used. The bottle was empty. David tried to remember how much his father-in-law had failed to swallow. *Perhaps half? More? But there was certainly brandy in the bottle when Isobel had wrestled it from her father.*

David said aloud, striving for certainty, "These glasses and the bottle were not on the coffee table when we went to bed. Right?"

There was no answer from the empty room.

Aloud, he said, struggling not to believe, "Somebody's been here. Somebody drank the old man's brandy."

He tried not to accept the evidence of his eyes. His first rational thought was that his father-in-law had returned. *Marion kicked him out again? The stupid old bugger! But two glasses? Why two glasses?*

David climbed the stairs quickly, but silently, his anger growing. At the spare room door, he took a deep breath before he opened the door quietly. The room was undisturbed, tidy and empty. He turned quickly at a sound behind him. Isobel was standing at their bedroom door.

"David?" she whispered, "What're you playing at?"

"I thought I heard a noise."

"Burglars?"

David shook his head.

"No. Sorry to disturb you."

He walked past her to the stair head.

"Where're you going now?"

"Drink of water."

"What's wrong with the bathroom?"

"Don't like bathroom water."

Isobel went back to bed and David went downstairs.

The French window into the garden was unlocked. David cursed aloud, but couldn't remember whether he had locked it when he came in from playing football with Jack. The television set and DVD player were still in place. The computer was undisturbed in the cubbyhole they called the study.

What the hell is going on? This doesn't make sense.

He walked out onto the patio and stared into the blindness of the night. No light shone from any neighbouring house. The moon was hiding behind fitful clouds. The night was silent, keeping its own secrets.

Wearing yellow Marigold gloves, David wrapped the bottle and tumblers separately in kitchen paper, placed each item in a carrier bag and enclosed all three items in a further carrier bag. In the morning he would take them to work. Freddie owed him a favour. He placed the package on the hall table.

When he turned around, Isobel was standing at the foot of the stairs.

She said, "Did you get your drink of water?"

"Yes, thanks."

"I won't ask why you're wearing my Marigolds," Isobel said.

"I can explain," David said.

Explain the unexplainable?

"You've found your feminine side?"

David made no response.

"You know where I keep my aprons. Help yourself."

"If I explained," David started to say.

"How are you on ironing?"

"Very funny."

"Are you coming to bed or not?"

"Yes."

Isobel started to walk upstairs, but turned to say, "I've laid out your best suit," and when her husband looked puzzled, "Isn't it that poor boy's funeral tomorrow? Today rather?"

David confessed, "I'd completely forgotten. Thank you."

He felt irrationally guilty as he followed Isobel upstairs.

"Are you going to bed in my marigolds?"

David turned back down the stairs, pulling off the gloves.

*

The now familiar images of the charity shop played before Cadet Timothy's eyes. He was reaching to switch it off as the big man and the dwarf left the shop when his mother called.

"Breakfast is on the table if you're interested!"

"Coming!"

He stretched to switch off the video and froze. He ran the video back and replayed the last scene, watching the intruders leave the charity shop. When the dwarf closed the door, he didn't switch off as Molly Brannigan and he had done before, but let the tape run on. Outside the shop, a car started to move, kangarooing as an inept driver attempted a U turn. The car was unmistakable. An ancient Morris Traveller. The cadet froze the tape.

"A Traveller! Somehow he's learned to drive. Monkey see, monkey do! But he takes any gear he can get. A Morris Traveller. Can't be many left now."

He ran the tape again and as the driver struggled to turn the car, strained to read the registration plate. In the poor light of the street lamp, Cadet Timothy thought he saw WMY.

"I'm putting your breakfast down for the dog when I count to ten. One! Two!"

The young man switched off the tape and ran for the stairs.

SIX

Fickle fortune waited until the funeral party reached the graveside before the heavens unleashed the monsoon. The grandparents were returned to the dreary graveyard chapel to develop pneumonia; the lesser of two evils. It rained throughout the burial service, steadily, remorselessly.

The drumbeat of rain on the coffin lid competed with the vicar's droning soliloquy. The harder the rain fell, the faster he recited the eternal clichés, anxious to escape as the words blurred on the page and his toes drowned in his socks. Only lifelong habit or a stubborn integrity kept the cleric at the graveside. Amy felt sorry for the old man and did her best to shelter him under her ridiculously tiny parrot-patterned parasol. Her mother and father stood stoically under the umbrella wielded by the young detective. Amy had decided he was wearing his best suit when he joined the family at the church. Now he looked like a drowned dog.

Amy thought, Why can't some referee blow a whistle and take the players off the pitch? Rain stops burial. Funeral to be resumed when the rain stops. Or postponed to a later date.

Suddenly she heard Paul laugh and felt her grief lift momentarily only for the enduring sorrow and loneliness to return;

Will it always be like this?

Paul's coffin was lowered into a deepening pool of water. The family dutifully threw handfuls of mud to splatter the coffin lid and leak away. The vicar with an inaudible final word fled the scene followed by the gravediggers plodding through the drowned grass. Mercifully, the rain slackened. For a long moment the family stood at the graveside unwilling, unable to leave. Derek Bowman was the first to move, encouraging his reluctant ex-wife towards the car. Amy followed with the detective. He's a nice guy, she thought, he could easily have stayed in the chapel.

As they walked back to the car, Amy saw a man standing in the trees, watching them. His presence disturbed her and memory awakening; she said to the detective, "I think I've seen that man before."

David Griffiths said, politely, "Where would that be?"

"I'm not sure. But I know it's important."

When she looked again the man had vanished. At the car they joined her mother while her father went to reclaim the grandparents.

"There was a man watching us, Mum."

Suddenly Amy saw the man beyond the trees, opening a car door. "There he is!"

As she spoke the man turned to look back at the funeral party.

Joyce Bowman said, "Of course! The hospital! The porter. How kind of him! In this rain too!"

But when the car started, Griffiths knew it wasn't kindness that had brought this man to the graveyard. The Morris Traveller started up noisily with a clashing of gears, kangarooed and moved away revving unnecessarily. To the Bowmans' surprise the young detective ran for his car.

"What an odd young man!" Joyce Bowman remarked, "Without a word!"

Amy said, "I think something important has just happened, Mum. Something we don't understand."

She found herself shivering, not entirely from cold, but assailed by a premonition of disaster.

"Get into the car," said her mother, "You're soaking! You should've used that parasol for yourself."

"Mum! He was an old man!"

"Young people die of pneumonia too!"

In the car Amy hugged a rug about herself weighed down with an awareness that Paul's death was not the end, but the beginning of something even more terrible.

*

Despite the Morris being driven badly, there was no opportunity to stop and question the driver in the busy Newcastle traffic. Griffiths decided to follow the porter to his destination. Other drivers were not so restrained when the Morris cut from lane to lane without any warning.

The Morris made an abrupt right hand turn across two lanes of traffic, narrowly avoiding collision with a bus and a car, into Convent Passage, a quiet avenue of tall Victorian houses.

"Ballcocks!" the detective cried aloud and braked.

As horns shrieked their protest at his behaviour, Griffiths was forced to drive on to the traffic lights where a similar protest greeted his U-turn in the face of oncoming cars.

"Sorry, sorry!" he apologised to the indignant headlights in the rear view mirror,

"God, they do it all the time on telly and nobody blinks an eye!"

There was no sign of the Morris in the avenue lined with parked cars.

"Perfect!" Griffiths cried, "Bloody perfect!"

Worse yet a bus blocked the carriageway dropping off and picking up passengers.

"You never heard of bus stops?" Griffiths complained aloud.

He stood on his horn and the bus ignored him. He had decided to get out and wave his warrant card about when the bus drove off giving a sardonic burp at his frustration.

As the bus departed the detective saw why the bus had blocked the carriageway. The Morris was parked on the bus stop and the man Joyce Bowman had identified as the hospital porter was walking away along the pavement. A car unexpectedly pulling out gave the detective the chance to park, breathing a thankful prayer. When he stepped out of the car, the porter was walking up the entry steps of a venerable three-storey house some two hundred yards ahead.

David Griffiths walked past the house to the corner and returned to walk casually up to the front door. The house was broken up into bedsits. As he studied the illegible names a woman came out of the front door and the detective slipped inside.

From a lower landing, Griffiths watched his quarry enter a door on the top floor. After a moment's indecision, the detective climbed the stairs and knocked on the door.

A man's voice replied, "The door is not locked. Please to enter."

Griffiths opened the door and stepped into a stonewalled room in a medieval castle. The shock was as if he were thrown into icy water. The detective could not breathe. Limbs and tongue were frozen. His heart sounded as a hammer in his head. He struggled to form words, but stood openmouthed in shock. Behind him he heard the door close.

In a wooden chair by an enormous fireplace wherein burned sweet-smelling logs sat a hard-faced woman in Stuart dress. At her shoulder stood the driver of the Morris Traveller. The key turned in the lock behind the detective. When he turned his head, a dwarf in chain mail, holding a cross bow, grinned slyly at him.

"What the hell's going on here?" said David Griffiths.

*

Joyce Bowman was half-heartedly watching television with the sound turned down because Amy was sleeping upstairs when someone began hammering on the front door.

Please, not you, Derek! And particularly not you drunk!

She opened the door to a white-faced David Griffiths.

"Is there something wrong?"

"I need you to come to the police station with me."

"Why?"

"Where's Amy?"

"She's asleep."

"Good. That's fine."

"Shall I wake her?"

"No. No. I just need you to come with me."

"But why would they need me?"

"They've arrested a man they need you to identify."

"Me? Why me?"

"Sorry. I just do what I'm told."

"Let me check on Amy."

Joyce Bowman turned away from the door, ignoring the detective's protests. *If I didn't know better I'd think he'd been drinking.*

"Please, hurry, doctor!" Griffiths called.

Joyce Bowman eased Amy's door open to find her daughter sleeping soundly.

She returned to the hallway where she was hustled out to the car.

"Are we really in such a hurry?" she complained, opening the passenger door.

The car drove off as she struggled to fasten her seat belt.

A figure stepped out of the shadow of the hedge and began to walk towards the house.

*

In the bedroom Amy stirred when a familiar voice called her name. "Amy? Wake up!"

Drowsy and barely awake, she sat up to stare at the figure framed in the doorway.

"Paul?"

Amy was abruptly awake as if she'd trodden on a live wire.

"Come on, Aimless! Come on! We've got to get out of this place! Hey, there's a good line for a song!"

"Paul?" she repeated, "Is it you? It can't be you. You're. Dead."

"It depends," said Paul, "what you mean by dead."

*

"You say they've arrested a man? But who is he?" Joyce Bowman demanded, "Do I know him?"

"I'm not allowed to say," said the detective.

They drove in a strained silence through the streets of Newcastle. When the first sign for Newcastle Airport appeared, Joyce Bowman asked, "The airport? What police station are we heading for?"

The detective ignored her question and overtook an Eddie Stobart lorry in the face of oncoming traffic. Joyce Bowman flinched. *My God,* she thought, *I thought we were dead then!*

"Stop the car," Joyce Bowman demanded, "I'm not going any farther until you tell me what's going on."

She saw a darkness in his face that frightened her.

"Please!" she said, "Please! I know something is terribly wrong. If you go on driving like this we'll have an accident."

Griffiths abruptly pulled the car over onto the hard shoulder and switched off the engine. The silence roared in their ears. Traffic buzzed past like angry bees.

Joyce Bowman said, "What's going on?"

The detective said, "They threatened to kill my family. Isobel and the children."

Uncomprehending, the doctor asked, "Who did? Who threatened them?"

The detective shook his head.

"I don't know."

"You must know! The Connollys?"

"I don't know. None of it makes any sense. I'm sorry. Please forgive me."

"Forgive you for what?"

When Griffiths pulled out the revolver and raised it to his head, a bewildered Joyce Bowman reacted instinctively. Restrained by the seat belt, she could only pull the young man towards her. The firing of the pistol inside the car was earsplitting.

When the ringing in her ears had begun to subside, Joyce Bowman said, "Are you alright?"

Griffiths nodded.

"Give me the gun."

The detective surrendered the revolver. Joyce Bowman broke the breech and opening the window, threw the cartridges into the grass. When Griffiths looked at her she said, "I have been a police surgeon," and put the pistol in the glove compartment.

Joyce Bowman said, "Why have you brought me out here?"

"They said to get you away from the house."

Realisation dawned in the doctor's eyes.

"Amy! They want Amy!"

The detective began to weep.

"I'm sorry. Really sorry. But they threatened to kill my children. What could I do?"

Joyce Bowman unlocked her seat belt.

"Get out," she commanded, and when he hesitated, "You're in no fit state to drive."

As Griffiths stumbled from the car, he asked, "What're you going to do with me?"

Joyce Bowman regarded the wretched man with both pity and contempt.

"That depends on whether my daughter is alive."

*

Spraying gravel, the car skidded to a halt in the drive. Joyce Bowman stumbled out and ran for the front door. The detective followed more slowly.

Joyce Bowman cried, "The front door is open!"

When she would have rushed inside, Griffiths took her arm.

"Let me go first. I owe you that much."

She saw he had the revolver in his hand.

Well, at least he can't shoot anybody.

Griffiths entered cautiously and the doctor followed, switching on the hallway lights.

"Amy! Amy?" Joyce Bowman called into the silence.

"Which is her room?" Griffiths asked.

They ran up the stairs together. The bedroom door stood open. Griffiths stood back as Joyce Bowman entered.

"She's not here!"

She gazed in horror at the bed where duvet and sheets had been ripped to pieces. Close to fainting, she sat down on the bedroom chair.

"It could be worse," Griffiths said.

Joyce Bowman almost laughed.

"How could it be worse?"

"There's no blood. She wasn't bleeding."

Struggling for control, the doctor agreed, "No, you're right. She wasn't bleeding. You're right. She's been abducted. Amy could still be alive."

SEVEN

In the bedroom Amy stirred when a familiar voice called her name.

"Amy? Wake up, Amy!"

Drowsy and barely awake she sat up to stare at the figure framed in the doorway.

"Paul?"

Amy was abruptly awake as if she'd trodden on a tin tack. Heart and breath stopped.

"Come on, Aimless! Come on! We've got to get out of this place! Hey, there's a good line for a song!"

"Paul?" she repeated, "Is it you? It can't be you. You're. Dead."

"It depends," said Paul, "what you mean by dead."

"I'm dreaming," Amy decided.

"The best sort of dream. The dream that isn't a dream."

"No," said Amy, smiling, shaking her head, "I'm dreaming. But I don't care.

What happens now?"

When Paul moved, she cried, "Don't go! Please let the dream last a little longer. You don't know how much I've missed you."

Paul came to sit on the bed.

"Can you feel my hand?"

Amy nodded; warm familiar fingers caressed her wrist.

"Can you see the scar where you handed me the knife and I wasn't looking?"

"Sorry," she said, "That was my fault."

"Can you feel the scar?" asked Paul.

Amy nodded and touched his face.

"Is it you? It can't be you. You're dead, Paul. Dead."

Her brother laughed and kissed her cheek.

"I know you're dead. We buried you."

"And I know you have a photograph of Colin Firth in your locker at school," Paul said, "Dead people don't know things like that."

He's alive, thought Amy, *it's not a dream. He's alive!*

"Where've you come from? What're you doing here?"

"That's not important. What matters now is that I'm here. You'll understand everything, but not now. But it's time we weren't here. Let's go!"

Amy, bewildered, resisted his urging arm.

"Go where?"

"Where we're needed."

"But we're needed here. Isn't Mum downstairs?"

"She's gone somewhere with the policeman."

"Then we must stay until she comes back. She'll want to see you."

Paul took his sister by the arm to move her from the bed.

"We can't wait. We must go now."

"Give me time to get dressed!"

"The nightdress will do. Nobody there will notice."

"There? Where's there?"

Paul mused, "If they did, they'd think it's a dress."

"I don't understand," cried Amy, "Who's they? Where's there?"

"Trust me. Do as I say. Come now! Please!"

Amy allowed herself to be led to the bedroom door and then Paul stopped, listening. The slightest of noises had caught his ear.

"What is it?"

"Shush! Listen! There's someone at the front door."

Amy laughed and said, "That'll be Mum!"

"No," said Paul, "It's not."

Amy tried to free herself, but Paul's grip tightened.

"That's Mum. She'll have a heart attack when she sees you."

Paul held her firmly, whispering, "Don't go to the door!"

Any complained, "Paul! Let me go! You're hurting me!"

"If it were Mum," Paul reasoned, "She has her key. It's not Mum."

Brother and sister tiptoed onto the landing. A dark shape could be seen through the glass panel in the front door. Amy reached for the light switch.

"Don't!" Paul commanded and Amy, surprised, obeyed.

"Then let me go down and open the door."

"It's not Mum," said Paul.

In a fearful silence they heard a scratching as of mice at the front door.

Paul reassured his sister, saying, "He's trying to pick the lock."

"Pick the lock?"

"He won't do it. He doesn't understand Chubb locks."

"I don't understand what's going on," Amy said, "But you're frightening me."

"He has to deal with physical things," Paul explained, "There are limits. He's a clever man, but he's not supernatural."

"Who isn't supernatural?"

Paul urged Amy on to the stairs, holding her arm.

"Come on, let's go!"

"Go where?" asked Amy, bewildered at the speed of events.

"Jethart," said Paul.

"Jethart?"

"Jedburgh. The Queen needs our help."

"What Queen?"

"Mary, Queen of Scots."

Amy gripped the banister to withstand his urgency.

"Paul, do'y'know what you're saying?"

"Do you remember the Stuart maid we saw in the garden?"

Amy nodded, suddenly flooded with the memory of the urgency of the maid's appeal.

"The Queen needs our help."

"Our help? What can we do for her? We're four hundred years too late."

"I don't know. I just know we're. Summoned. Yes, that's the word. We've been summoned.

In a breathless silence the teenagers slid down the stairs, and around the staircase into the kitchen. Holding the door ajar Paul and Amy watched the shadow at the front door.

"I can hear you breathing," Amy said, "It can't be a dream."

From outside the door came a frustrated man's muffled curse.

"Who is it at the door?"

"Bothwell," Paul explained in a whisper.

"Who?"

"James Hepburn, Earl of Bothwell."

"Queen Mary's lover?"

"Not her lover, Amy. Her bitterest enemy."

Amy's rational mind suddenly mutinied and she cried, "It isn't true. It can't be. I won't believe it. This is the twenty-first century. Two thousand and twelve, for God's sake! There is no sixteenth century Scottish warlord at our front door. I'm dreaming a terrible dream. Before it gets any worse, I'm going back to bed."

Paul held his sister tightly, whispering fiercely, "James Hepburn, Third Earl of Bothwell, died in a Danish prison. Supposedly mad as a hatter. Raving of horseless carriages and silver dragons that ate the sky. Moving pictures in boxes and sticks that talked. Does any of that sound familiar to you?"

A panel in the front door shattered. Glass dropped into the hall.

"He's lost patience," Paul whispered.

A hand reached in and the front door opened. A shapeless figure entered. The light from the street caught his face. Amy would've called out if Paul had not his hand across her mouth: a solid, warm, fleshy hand, smelling of brother. Paul's real. *Not dead*, thought Amy, *therefore, Q.E.D., this is all happening. James Hepburn, Earl of Bothwell, has travelled through time and is standing at the foot of our stairs..*

Amy would have laughed, but Paul, sensing hysteria, pulled her backwards into the doubtful security of the kitchen. When she struggled for breath, Paul released his grip.

In the tiniest of whispers Amy asked, "What's he doing here?"

"He's come to kill you."

Amy's heart stopped.

"If all this is real. If he has come through time. And I must be mad to believe you. Why would a man from the sixteenth century want to kill me?"

"To finish the business."

"What business?"

"Only the Gemini can help the Queen."

"Gemini?"

"Twins sharing the same birth date as the Queen. You and I."

Amy stood within Paul's grasp trying to make sense of what was happening.

"He's going upstairs," Paul whispered, "We must go."

He turned the kitchen door key slowly, silently.

Once out of the drive they began to run. Upstairs in thirty-nine, Wellington Terrace, the man who came to murder Amy, found the bedroom empty and in a fury began to slash at the bedclothes.

Hand in hand, the teenagers ran down the street, fleeting shadows flying from one pool of light to the next. Unseeing, they raced past a parked Morris Traveller where a dark shape stirred at the sound of running feet and a head rose above the passenger door. Cymian slid from the car and began to follow the twins.

*

Cadet Timothy was wheeling his bicycle into the station yard when he saw D.C. Susan Duffy crossing to a patrol car.

"D.C. Duffy!" he shouted, and ran towards her, hampered by his bicycle. Susan Duffy ignored him and got into the car. The cadet caught the door as she tried to close it and said, "I have something important to tell you!"

He became aware of D.S. Mitchell in the driver's seat.

"Somebody stole your dinner money? There, there, never mind!"

Susan laughed, reclaimed the door and said, "Another time. Robbery in progress."

Mitchell hit the accelerator. The car leapt across the yard and vanished into the traffic, siren blaring. The cadet's last sight of Susan Duffy was of her struggling to fasten her safety belt. He felt hurt he had been ignored. They were the adults and he was the kid.

"Then I'll sort it without you," he promised himself.

*

At the ramp to the multi-storey car park, Amy baulked as Paul tugged at her hand.

"Come on, Amy!"

"What're we doing here?"

The dark mouth of the behemoth frightened Amy. *This is not right. This is so not right.*

"Trust me," Paul assured her, "I know what I'm doing."

"Something is wrong," Amy persisted, "If you are really here you would know it. We've always known when things are iffy."

"Oh, ye of little faith," Paul rebuked his sister, "Never mistake the manifestation for the reality."

"And what does that mean?"

"Nothing is what it seems," said Paul, "The old rules don't apply."

Amy hesitated still, plagued by a nagging doubt.

"Come on, we're expected," Paul insisted, tugging at her wrist to pull her up the ramp.

"Hang on, let me get my breath back. I've a stitch."

"A stitch," said Paul, and laughed, "A stitch in time. That's what's wrong.

The stitches in time."

Amy shook her head.

"I don't understand."

"The stitches are giving way," said Paul, "The threads are breaking."

Amy glimpsed how frightened her brother was.

Well, we're together. That's the good thing.

His face darkened.

"Never mistake the manifestation for the reality," he recited.

If this is a dream, thought Amy, *or real, something terrible is going to happen.*

"This is a car park," said Amy, "that's the reality."

"Unless it's simply a manifestation. And the reality is deeper."

"Are we driving to Jedburgh? Because if we are, you haven't a license."

Even as she spoke Amy thought, *How silly! You don't need licences in dreams. If this is a dream.*

"We don't need a car. Come on!"

The dark mouth of the concrete cavern threatened Amy and she resisted his urgent hand.

"I'm not going in there until you give me an explanation. An explanation I can understand. I'm frightened, Paul. Something's very wrong. Can't you feel it?"

Her brother embraced her, his soothing arms lessening her anxiety.

"Don't be afraid. We're nearly there."

"Where?"

"Without time there is nowhere and no when. No now and no then."

"I don't want riddles, Paul."

"What's the name of this car park?"

Amy stared into the sombre darkness of the concrete canyon.

"The Castle. What's that got to do with it?"

"Everything."

"Paul, the castle isn't here anymore."

"Isn't it? Don't mistake the manifestation."

"Stop saying that," Amy commanded, "There's something wrong here. Can't you feel it? Something really bad."

Something has happened to Paul, thought Amy, *he can't hear what I can hear. We always knew. He's deaf.*

Paul laughed reassuringly, saying, "There's nothing wrong. Everything's all right. Come on, let's go!"

Reluctantly, Amy allowed herself to be drawn into the concrete barren and up the windy ramp to the first floor into its empty echoing space, stinking of oil and petrol. Errant wind rattled a drink can across the concrete. Amy hesitated at the second flight of urine-stinking stairs, but Paul's commanding grasp drew her up to another aimless concrete plain. And yet up again and again as Amy's fear ballooned into certainty. Her breath came hastily, anxiously, her fear sprouting legs. *Can you not sense it, Paul? They're here somewhere. Waiting to kill us.* But Paul seemed deaf to her fear.

They emerged, Paul almost dragging Amy onto the final concrete desert with the starless sky above and the city lights below. *There's no wind. How strange? She was very afraid.*

"Now where?" asked Amy. There was nowhere to go.

"The door I seek is there," Paul said.

"Where?"

Amy stared about her in bewilderment.

"There," said Paul, pointing to a bulkhead, but Amy could see nothing but stained concrete.

Suddenly she was chilled by alien laughter. Sitting on the outer curtain wall was Cymian, swinging his legs.

Oh, God, has Paul brought me here to be killed?

"There's many a slip, cousins," said the little man, "between cup and lip."

He whistled shrilly and from the dark mouth of the opposing ramp emerged a wolfish band in iron and leather, swords and axes catching the light.

Amy cried out in fear, holding tightly to Paul's hand.

"Sorry, Amy. You were right. Too much ahead of myself."

"What answer has you to cold steel, young sir?" enquired the dwarf.

Amy felt Paul tense beside her and freed her hand.

"No answer? A pity! Then for all your cleverness, we'll chop you up and down for pie-meat and none'll be the wiser."

The dwarf clapped his hands and the wolves began to circle the twins, swords drumming on targes, axes swinging in widening arcs.

As the circle began to close Paul stepped in front of his sister.

"Run, Amy," he hissed, "Run for your life! Now!"

To the reivers he shouted, "Let her go! She has not yet begun!"

He pushed Amy away towards the ramp they had climbed.

"Run! Before it's too late!"

He pleaded with the advancing wolves, "She is no threat to you!"

For a moment the reivers hesitated, looking to the dwarf for guidance.

To Cymian, Paul shouted, "You have me. I'm all you need. The circle is broken.

The Queen cannot be redeemed. Let the girl go! Let my death be an end to it!"

Cymian laughed and danced in glee, relishing his surrender.

To his sister, Paul cried, "Run, Amy! Run for your life!"

But her legs would not obey. She stood frozen as the circle closed behind her.

The dwarf laughed and danced in delight on the curtain wall.

"You lie," cried Cymian, "You lie, master! The maid has begun. She is here and therefore, begging your pardon in contradictory-wise, she has begun! 'tis clear she has begun. And here she shall be ended! As will yourself, master! As you will shortly see!"

Cymian mocked the twins and capered on the wall to the enjoyment of the reivers. *Humpty-dumpty sat on the wall,* thought Paul, *tensing himself for a desperate attempt, Humpty-dumpty had a great fall.* But the dwarf reading his intention jumped down. *There are limits, thought Paul, they are constrained.*

Amy looked around at the wolves in chain mail who mocked and threatened her.

Oh, please, God, let this be a dream. Please let me wake up in my own bed. Now. Right now. I'll be a good girl forever. I promise. And then she thought, But if this is a dream then Paul would be dead. And I will be alone again. Better we both die here together.

Aloud she cried, "If this is not a dream, be quick and let me die!"

"Dying's no easier than being born, mistress," said the dwarf, as if reading her mind, "but I'll serve you short measure if you steps my way."

Amy walked towards Cymian and the bare blade.

*

Detective Constable Susan Duffy stood at D.I. Harold Starling's open office door.

The lamplight reflected from his balding head as he read from the file. Susan tapped on the door and the D.I. looked up.

"Yes?"

"Have you got a minute, sir?"

D.I. Harold Starling sighed.

"Come in, Duffy."

Susan entered the office, but wasn't invited to sit down. She opened a file from the stack she carried.

"Haven't you finished the stats yet?"

"That's what I wanted to see you about, sir."

"Go on."

It was the least inviting invitation Susan had ever received.

"It doesn't make sense. Well, it doesn't fit the pattern. Any pattern."

"What doesn't make sense?"

The Inspector sounded both irritated and tired. Not for the first time Susan wondered if he was the right man to lead the squad. *Maybe we'd be more efficient if he held the loyalty of the officers?*

Susan hesitated and said, "This isn't our usual pattern. At least it isn't to me."

"What isn't?"

"Too many people are dying. The boy in the road accident. The nurse in the hospital. Heart attack apparently. On the ward at about the same time as the old woman, Missis Margaret Foulkes. The teacher in the river. Suicide."

"So?"

"All in some way connected to the same ward on Armstrong Memorial where the sister of the dead boy had been in a coma."

"What's the connection with the teacher?"

"Gabrielle Oporto. She was working at the hospital. Supporting young people."

"So she got fed up and jumped from a bridge."

"Filling her pockets and trousers with stones to make sure she didn't come up again?"

"Sensible girl."

"Breaking her neck before she jumped?"

D.I. Harold Starling held out a hand for the file. Susan struggled with her burden and handed him a slim file. Starling scanned the file and handed it back.

"Hit something on the bridge or in the water. Half the nicked motors are in the Tyne."

"She didn't drown," said Susan.

D.I. Harold Starling shook his head.

"Not significant."

"She was dead before she went into the water," Susan insisted.

"Anything else?"

"Missis Foulkes was due to return home in a few days. Recovered well from her operation."

"How old?"

Susan checked the file.

"Had her seventy-ninth birthday in hospital."

D.I. Harold Starling shrugged.

"Good for her! Anything else?"

"Could I ask you to look at that videotape from the charity shop, sir? In her statement Amy Bowman says."

D.I. Harold Starling interrupted to say, "It's been binned."

Detective Constable Duffy stared at her superior in bewilderment.

"But you said it was in the system?"

"Well, now it's not."

Susan struggled not to speak. *You really are as stupid as you look! You could've given me the tape. But no!*

"That's it then?"

Susan nodded.

"Stats on my desk nine sharp tomorrow. Now buzz off!"

Susan hesitated in the doorway.

"Yes?"

"When did you bin the tape, sir?"

"Close the door as you go."

Susan quietly closed the office door. She waited until she was in the squad room and placed the files on her desk before she screamed. The only occupant, the oldest detective, Bill Malpas said, "Let me guess? Our Harold?"

Susan nodded.

"You think he doesn't like you?"

Susan nodded, not trusting herself to speak.

"Fact is, he doesn't like women, period. Fact is, you're smarter than he is. And that frightens him shitless."

Susan smiled at the older man. She had a certain affection for him.

On their first op together, a drugs raid, Susan had been hit in the face. Bill Malpas, as he cleaned the wound, offered advice.

"Next time, lass, get your retaliation in first."

"But that's not fair," was Susan's naïve reply and a surprised Bill Malpas had stopped dabbing away blood, to say, "Fair? There is no 'fair' dealing with scum! Kick him in the goolies before he decks you."

"When do the bin men come, Bill?"

"Think I heard them this morning. You lost something?"

"I'm not sure. I think it was important. Or it could be nothing. I don't know."

What I do know is those two men are dangerous.

EIGHT

It seemed as if the traffic lights had locked on red. Joyce Bowman swore softly, aware of the young woman sitting beside her. As if to shut out her presence, Joyce switched on the radio only to hear the local newsreader say, "Today police were called to the Castle car park where an early morning commuter was shocked to discover…"

The young reporter switched off the radio. Joyce Bowman stared into the rainswept windscreen at the immobile traffic. *It's curious, but I feel nothing. I'm numb. No pain. No grief. Nothing. Is this how a soldier feels after bloody combat? I can't even cry. Why can't I cry?*

"You're in shock," the young woman said, "Would it help if you talked to me?"

Joyce Bowman said, "It was a mistake letting you into the car. I thought as a woman I might be able."

The horns of all the world's traffic snarled at once.

"It's green," said the young reporter, and Joyce recovered herself sufficiently to engage gear and drive across the junction.

"I'd rather not talk to any reporter," said Joyce to the windscreen, "I thought I might talk to you. Rather than all of them. Because you're a woman. But it was a mistake."

"I'm not going to ask stupid questions about how does it feel," the young woman said sympathetically, "because I couldn't possibly understand how it feels."

"I don't feel anything, "Joyce said, "Is there something wrong with me?"

She felt the young woman shake her head.

"Why can't I cry?"

"Doctor Bowman," said the young reporter, "Mister Brian Connolly says the allegations your husband…"

"We're divorced," said Joyce, avoiding two cyclists seemingly intent on suicide.

"The allegation your ex-husband is making that someone in Mister Connelly's family is responsible for the death of your son is false. He completely denies any suggestion of violence. Although he believes you were responsible for the death of his daughter and grandchild. What do you say?"

Joyce Bowman said, "I am not responsible for the death of his daughter and her baby. I think he would do better to consider her history of addiction."

"Mister Connelly says you've shown no consideration for his situation."

Doctor Bowman laughed bitterly, glancing into the earnest face of the young woman.

"Really? And I'm on my way to tell her father that our daughter, Amy, has been found dead, murdered, in a car park?"

The young reporter had nothing to say. Doctor Bowman brought the car to a stop.

"I'm sorry. I'm going to drop you here. Sorry. It was a mistake."

The young woman opened the passenger door and climbed out.

"Thank you, Doctor Bowman. I'm so sorry."

Joyce sat and watched the young woman walk away. *This is so weird,* she thought, *I feel nothing. It's all as if it's happening to someone else. Nothing is real.*

*

Cadet Timothy was finishing his burger and fries in the canteen when W.P.C. Melanie Ford came to his table. When he looked up he blushed. He always blushed in the presence of this young woman and damned himself for blushing. It was a struggle to remember the fair damsel he worshipped from afar was a police officer and a colleague. Not a fantasy.

"Hi, John," she said, smiling upon his roseate complexion, "Your D.C. Duffy's on schools so I'll give it to you."

The police cadet nodded. *Give me what? Your heart? Love eternal?*

"Duffy wanted to know the whereabouts of a certain Morris Traveller?"

Cadet Timothy sat bolt upright, pushing away his plate. *Thank God she didn't find Duffy!*

"Yes. Morris Traveller. Part registration WMY?"

"She just wanted location? No action?"

"That's right."

Melanie Ford read from her yellow sheet.

"WMY 675G. First registered June, 1969. Historic vehicle. Currently parked in the layby at Old Sally, Wall Street."

"Old Sally?"

"You're not Newkie, are you?"

"No," he admitted sadly. *Just a prat from Peterlee.*

"Wall Street? What's left of the city wall? Old Sally? There was a city gate there once, but it's blocked now. Okay?"

The cadet nodded understanding.

"The traffic boys want to know-."

The cadet interrupted to say, "Duffy's on to something. Just leave it alone?"

"Okay!" agreed Melanie, "Hope it works out."

She smiled sweetly and turned away; then stopped and turned to the cadet again.

She's going to ask if I'd like to accompany her to-

"I hope you don't mind," she said and his heart beat like a bass drum, "But you've got ketchup on your tunic."

John Timothy watched Melanie cross the canteen to the exit where she turned smiling and waved her fingers at him. Cadet Timothy's face bloomed rosier than any apple.

He felt guilty that he hadn't passed on what he had learned from running the tape to Susan Duffy. *But I want to do something to show I'm not altogether useless.*

He unlocked his bike in the station yard and pedalled off to find Old Sally, Wall Street. A sense of guilt nagged at him.

*

There was a wide green with three horse chestnut trees between the main carriageway of Wall Street and the remaining city wall with its still visible, but blocked Sally gate. Cadet Timothy dismounted from his bike and left it leaning against the first horse chestnut while he went to inspect the Morris Traveller, registration WMY 675G.

On the front passenger seat there was a feather boa and a baseball cap. The rear area had been folded down and the space created was filled with boxes of wine bottles and cases of lager. The big man and the dwarf had visited another shop after closing time. There were two empty bottles and a number of empty lager cans. The cadet noted three cans had been opened by stabbing with a sharp implement, but others had been ring-pulled. With a sudden insight, Timothy realised someone had learned to use the ring pull. This was an insight with disturbing echoes.

The cadet turned from the car and saw someone was sitting at the foot of the second tree. An old, unshaven man was drinking from a lager can. The number of empty cans around him demonstrated he had been imbibing for some time. Timothy could smell his stink as he approached closer. The alkie was dressed in an old army greatcoat, torn and dirty jeans and foul trainers.

Cadet Timothy said, "You taught him how to use the ring pull, didn't you?"

"That's no agin the law," said the alkie.

"Which one? Which one didn't know what to do?"

"The wee man. He was stabbing at the cans. Sich a waste! Breaking me heart he was."

"And he gave you those cans?"

"Aye, there's still them that knows kindness."

"Which way did they go?"

The alkie waved his arms about.

"One minute they're here. Then they're gone."

"They? The big man was here?"

"Divvent yee get on the wrong side of him, son," warned the alkie, momentarily sober, "Yee do and he'll tear ya arms off!"

"You do know it's an offence to be drunk in public?"

"Haddaway!" cried the alkie, "You's no a real pollis!"

Cadet Timothy settled to watch the Traveller. The alkie drank, sang and finally fell asleep. The young man was stretching his cramped legs when something beyond belief happened. A big bearded man in leather jacket and trousers walked out through the stone-blocked sally gate and went to the car. The cadet struggled to accept the evidence of his own eyes and then his training took over. Cadet Timothy walked over to the big man who was bending into the Traveller and asked, "Are you the owner of this car, sir?"

The big man straightened up slowly and turned upon the young man a face of such evil intent that the cadet took a step back, but recovered himself to say, "I have reason to believe this is not your car, sir. And that you have been involved in at least one burglary."

The big man threw back his head and laughed aloud.

"This is no laughing matter, sir."

"Indeed it is," said the big man, "And it will be the death of you!"

The young man felt the most agonising pain in his lower back. He stumbled and turned to find the dwarf grinning at him, a bloody stiletto in his hand.

"You stabbed me!" the cadet cried, disbelievingly.

"And so again!" smiled the dwarf and leapt upon him to plunge the stiletto into his chest.

Cadet John Timothy died with a look of utter astonishment on his face.

Bothwell and Cymian dragged the young man's body through the sally port and vanished from the sight of mortal men. Two feral teenagers rode off on the bicycle and the alkie slept on under the afternoon sun.

*

The grizzled sergeant, escorting Doctor Bowman through the custody area, said, "We're all very sorry for your loss."

Joyce knew it was a cliché he'd learnt from an American television drama, but when she looked into his face she saw he was telling the truth.

"Thank you. Have you got him locked up?"

The sergeant looked embarrassed.

"He's promised to behave himself."

Joyce said, "That'll be a first."

Walking down the stairs together, Joyce asked, "What exactly has he done?"

At the foot of the stairs the sergeant explained, "He went to Connolly's betting shop and asked to see Brian Connolly. When he was refused, he attacked the staff."

"Good God!" said Joyce, "That doesn't sound like him."

As they walked along the gloomy corridor the sergeant, with a certain grudging respect, said, "Fought his way through three men to reach Connolly's office."

"But why?"

"To warn him he will find out who killed his son and abducted-."The sergeant faltered, "He doesn't know his daughter is dead."

They stopped outside the third cell.

"Are you going to tell him, doctor?"

Joyce nodded.

The sergeant said, "Connolly isn't pressing charges. You can take him home once the formalities are completed."

The key rattled in the lock and the cell door creaked open. *It's like being in a film,* thought Joyce Bowman, *nothing is real.*

Derek Bowman was sitting on the concrete bed. He was in his shirtsleeves. He was lacking a tooth and his face was bruised. There was blood on his face and shirt. He looked up at Joyce and said, "They locked me up! Can you imagine that?"

The sergeant said, "Not for much longer, Mister Bowman. You're going home. I'll leave you with your wife for a minute or two. There'll be papers to sign."

Joyce Bowman sat beside her estranged husband. She took his hand and looked into his sad, defiant face.

"I mean what I said. I will kill him."

Without warning, Joyce Bowman felt herself overwhelmed with grief. She cried aloud and wept as her world crumbled and fell. She knew the pain of loss would never leave her. When she turned to Derek she saw the same despair in his eyes and cried out in her torment. There was no coherent thought. No comfort could reach her and she clung to the man as if the ocean's tide would tear her away.

"What is it?" asked Derek Bowman, "What's happened?"

The man embraced her, held her close, soothed her, wiped at her tears, not knowing, but knowing she was going to tell him something most terrifying.

"What is it?" he repeated, "What's happened? Oh, my God, is it Amy?"

Joyce Bowman found the strength to say, "They've killed her."

The man was unbelieving.

"Killed her? Why would they do that?"

Joyce Bowman shook her head, knowing no answers.

"They found her this morning on the top floor of the Castle car park."

"Car park? In God's name, why would they kill the child?"

Derek Bowman began to weep. Joyce sat next to, but a hundred miles away from her ex-husband.

Now am I in hell, thought Joyce, *and never will I be out of it.*

In the corridor the sergeant heard the man weeping and turned away, papers in hand.

*

When Amy walked towards the dwarf he retreated, surprised and then recovered, sheathing his blade. Shaking out a noose, he called, "Come to me, sweetling! I have a necklace that will serve you well."

The reivers laughed as if this were some splendid jest.

"How will you reach my neck, manikin?" Amy taunted the little man and all humour left his face.

When the reivers laughed at his discomfort, Cymian snarled at them and they fell silent. Amy felt Paul behind her, drawing her away, whispering in her ear, "Run down the stairs. Run back to the twenty-first century. Time is still time there."

They retreated, hand in hand, edging towards the dark stairs, watching the circling, jeering clansmen.

"This wasn't supposed to happen," Paul said, "Go now before it's too late."

Amy shook her head.

"Not without you," she said, "Not now I've found you."

Amy smiled into her brother's desperate face.

"If I'm going to die, at least I'm with you," she said, but she was very much afraid.

Paul shouted at Cymian, "Let her go! You have me. The Gemini are parted. Nothing can save the Queen now. Let her go!"

The reivers catcalled and jeered, banging swords on shields and the triumphant dwarf cried, "She shall not go! She dies here! And I shall have the privilege of choking the life from her. Then the Gemini are done! And my master is the victor!"

Paul pushed Amy towards the stairs, but she clung to his arm.

"I'm not leaving you!" she cried.

Then, with a lurch that threw them both from their feet and tangled reivers' swords and shields, the top deck of the Castle car park became the garden of the Jethart House, the lawns running down to the banks of the Jedwater. Lights shone in the upper windows of the House.

Paul and Amy slowly regained their feet gazing about them in bewilderment. The starless sky of what had been twenty-first century Newcastle was ablaze with stars and a full silver moon. *Boys and girls come out to play, the moon doth shine as bright as day,* thought Amy and laughed.

Cymian and the reivers, bewildered, turned towards a tumult of voices from the House as soldiers armed with halberds and swords ran towards them shouting. The charge from the House broke up the reivers' hasty stand. Halberds reached and struck beyond sword's length. The clash of metal rang harsh. One man fell and a reiver fled, grasping a near-severed arm. Paul pulled Amy from the battle melee. A man screamed as he died. Another stood gaping at a mortal wound.

A woman's voice called. An astonished Amy saw it was the Stuart maid, standing by the House as on the day the twins first visited Jedburgh. A ladder ran up to a door on the first floor. The outer staircase had been destroyed. It was a house under siege. There were women's faces in the open doorway. The marie at the ladder's foot, called urgently, "Run! Run quickly! For mercy's sake, come to me, milord, milady!"

As the twins turned to flee to the House, Cymian ran to catch Amy. Paul saw the fear in the marie's face and turning, found the dwarf within a sword's reach. Amy saw about her the ugly image of an earlier world.

Soldiers and reivers were locked in combat, striking at each other, screaming hatred and fear. A man fell mortally stricken. Another fell to his knees clasping his face. Urgent voices called from the House as fresh reivers ran up from the river.

"Quickly, quickly, oh, my lord, my lady!" the marie cried.

Terror in her face, the marie began to mount the ladder. Paul, aware of death on their heels, ran blindly, trailing a hand behind, reaching for his sister's failing grasp. Then Amy was gone.

The dwarf caught Amy by the legs and brought her down, triumphantly sitting astride her, tightening the assassin's cord about her neck. Amy struggled, choking, throttled, to throw him off. Paul turned about, as in a dream, running through treacle, to help Amy. *Too late!* cried the dwarf's triumphant face.

Then a young man broke from the general melee and struck the dwarf across the head with shaft of a broken pike. Iron cap flying, Cymian collapsed like a rag doll. The young man snatched up Amy, tumbling her across his shoulder, urging Paul back towards the House.

"Quickly, lord, quickly!" the young man cried, pushing Paul up the ladder before him.

When Paul hesitated the young man cried, "Climb or die, lord! I have the lady!"

Paul, panting, climbed to the young marie who dragged him into the doorway to collapse on the floor. The young man gasping, stumbled in with Amy on his shoulder. Amy stood within his embrace, bewildered with a storm of voices about her. When she saw the young man's scalp was bleeding, she fainted. *How absurd,* was her last thought, *it isn't real.*

In the garden a horn blew. Harried by a roar from the reivers, the survivors of the sally party tumbled up the ladder into the upper hall. At the ladder foot the last soldier, a giant of a man, stood, holding off the invaders. With a final sweeping blow of his axe, he scrambled up the ladder, striking, kicking behind him, to fall into the doorway. As the first reiver struggled to reach the doorsill, a soldier thrust a halberd into his throat and he fell, artery spouting blood, upon the heads of his comrades. The household jeered as he fell, the ladder was hauled inboard and the door was slammed shut as the first crossbow bolts struck wood and stone. For a long moment, a silence fell upon the

House as friends looked around anxiously for friends and wounds were disclosed.

Then voices and laughter began. Soldiers dispersed over the floor of the banqueting hall to examine wounds, attend one another, laugh, shout and boast.

"Thanks be to the good Lord, that you are safely come," the young marie said to Paul, slumped, back against the wall, his legs sprawling on the elm boards.

"Safely?" cried Paul in anguish for the wounded in House and the dead on the grass below the House.

"Is my sister all right?"

"She is but swooned."

The young man who carried Amy to safety removed the assassin's thong from about her neck, anxiously watching her pale face.

"She breathes," he said and smiled, "All is well."

*

On the open roof of the Castle car park the ambulance men lifted the body of Amy Bowman onto the stretcher and into the ambulance. Doctor, S.O.C.O and police officers stood watching. The ambulance drove away and the team began to disperse. Only a solitary constable was left to guard the fluttering plastic tape. On the outer curtain wall a jackdaw alighted to study the policeman with a wary eye and then, certain sure of his harmlessness, fluttered down to parade the concrete.

Detective Constable Susan Duffy stood within the palisade of tape looking down at, but not seeing the oil stained concrete where Amy Bowman died.

"What on earth were you doing here?" Susan cried aloud, "Did you die here? Or were you dumped here? Neither makes any sense."

NINE

"Do you know these people?" Amy whispered to Paul.

They were sitting at the fireplace in the great hall of the House. The Queen's chair, bearing its banner *In My End is My Beginning* was empty of its royal occupant.

"Sort of. The marie is Mary Seton."

Amy recited, "Mary Seton, Mary Beaton, Mary Fleming and Mary Livingston. The four maries."

Three ladies looked up from their tasks among the soldiers and smiled.

Paul said, "I was lying in the road."

Amy interrupted to say, "You were dead."

"Mary Seaton came to me and brought me here."

"How?" asked Amy.

"I don't really understand," Paul explained, "Mary said."

"Take my hand," said Mary Seton, standing before them offering pewter tankards. Amy and Paul took the drinks, sniffed at the hot mixture and sipped.

"'Tis a herbal toddy," Mary Seaton said, sitting down beside the twins, "It will warm your insides and cheer the spirit."

"Thank you," said Amy. Brother and sister drank.

"I said, take my hand and Lord Paul said, 'Where are we going?'" The marie laughed.

"It seemed I was falling forever through darkness, but I knew I must keep hold of that hand. And then I was here."

"Then the Lord Paul was sent back to bring you here, lady."

"But why?" asked Amy.

"Because it is the hour of the Gemini and Her Majesty is in the gravest danger of death."

A young man approached out of the cheerful assembly in the hall.

Mary said, "May I introduce Adam Blackwood, Her Majesty's Writer?"

"Secretary?" suggested Paul and the young man nodded.

Amy knew at once it was Adam Blackwood who had rescued her from the dwarf, but was distinctly uncomfortable as he bent to one knee before her.

"You rescued me," Amy cried, "The dwarf would've killed me."

"I beg pardon for being so familiar," Adam Blackwood pleaded.

"I owe you my life," said Amy.

"It was my pleasure. Let us hope it is never necessary again, milady."

Amy vowed, "I'll never be able to thank you enough."

"To see the Gemini here together is enough recompense," responded the Queen's secretary.

As they sat and sipped the toddy, Amy noted Paul was right. Her plain cotton nightdress was not altogether dissimilar to the maries' dresses. Paul's leather jacket and jeans raised no comment. Leather jerkins were common among the men of the household.

"You seem to have expected us," Amy ventured.

"That is so," smiled Mary Seton.

"Although not knowing the hour," Adam said.

"But how did you know?" Paul asked, "And why us? Yes, we're twins, but there's nothing remarkable about us."

Mary and Adam laughed.

"Forgive us! But you are the Gemini. There have been other times. But all ended in failure. This time you will succeed."

"I have long dreamt of your coming," Mary said, "I was assured that you were in passage. Then I saw you."

Adam commented, "We kept good watch and awaited you. Knowing not the hour, but keeping good ward and watch."

Paul and Amy exchanged glances of puzzlement.

"But why are we here?"

"That is yet to be revealed," Adam stated confidently.

"Where is her Majesty?" Amy asked.

"Her Majesty is abed, lady," Mary said, "When you are refreshed, you will be taken into her presence."

"We are refreshed," Paul suggested and Amy agreed.

Preceded by Mary Seaton bearing a torch and followed by the Secretary who had attached himself to Amy, the twins climbed the stairs to the Queen's chamber.

Paul and Adam waited on the landing as Amy and Mary entered. The bed and the room were draped with mourning. The air was stifling and Amy struggled to breathe. A priest chanted monotonously in a corner of the chamber. When the draperies were drawn aside from the bed Amy saw a young woman, heavily pregnant, exhausted by a fruitless labour, lying comatose, scarcely breathing.

"I never realized how young she was-is," said Amy, struggling to grasp the reality, "And how like me!"

Mary said, "You might be sisters, lady."

The Queen stirred in her bed, opened her eyes, and through dry lips tried to speak. Amy took the sponge from the bowl and moistened her lips.

"Help me," croaked the Queen, "Give me ease for pity's sake."

"What's wrong?" Amy cried to the marie.

"She cannot give birth."

"Where's the midwife? The doctor?"

The marie shook her head.

"There is no physician here to ease her."

"But she's the Queen!" cried Amy.

"Lord Bothwell will let no one come or go."

"But why would he do that? To put the Queen in such danger?"

"He intends the child shall die here. And if God so wills, the Queen also."

"But the King? Why does he not come to her aid?"

The marie shook her head sadly.

"He is of no account. A useless ninny who wishes her Majesty dead," said Mary Seton, "But now that you are come, all will be well."

Amy stared at the marie blankly.

Mary smiled serenely, "Now, praise God, all will be well. The babe will be born and the Queen shall live."

The girl's simple faith left Amy speechless. When she found her tongue she said, falteringly, "Mary, who do you think we are?"

The marie laughed, "Are you not Angels then? Come to deliver her Majesty?"

Amy laughed, not in amusement, but near-hysteria, yet the laughter seemed to reassure Mary.

"Then surely all will be well?"

"I hope so. I truly hope you're right."

"I saw you in my dream, lady," the marie said, "And now you are here. All will be well. I know it to be so."

Amy struggled to grasp this reality, an alien reality lit by torches and candles in the stifling-hot chamber of a long-dead Queen, a chamber that stank of ordure and death.

"Why can't she give birth?" Amy asked, "What is wrong?"

Mary Seton moved to put aside the sheet, but Amy stayed her hand.

"The babe is upside down," Mary said, "Where the head would be there is a leg."

Amy struggled with the dawning horror. *If the baby isn't already dead, it is dying and dying will kill the Queen.*

"The midwife," Amy insisted, "Her Majesty must've had a midwife. Where is she?"

"When she saw the babe was obstructed," the girl recounted sadly, "she left the House. She told no one but left the House."

"She ran away?"

Mary Seton nodded.

"And there's no doctor? No surgeon for the soldiers?"

The marie shook her head.

"There must be a doctor, a midwife, in Jethart?"

"No one may approach the House. On fear of death."

"For God's sake!" cried Amy, "Is there no one to help the Queen?"

Mary Seton looked at Amy in surprise.

"You are here, milady," she smiled, "It is well that you have come."

"Me?" cried Amy, in cold panic, "What can I do?"

"But you have come in answer to our prayers, milady," Mary cried, puzzled, bewildered, "You are the Gemini."

"The baby cannot be born like that," Amy despaired, "It must be turned. It will die. If it isn't already dead. And then if she doesn't have medical attention, Her Majesty will die very soon. A horrible death."

What nightmare have we fallen into? A dead baby and a dying Queen?

"Then command and we shall obey," said Mary Seton.

"Command? To do what? It's all too late."

Amy laughed bitterly.

"Any moment now I'll wake up and everything will be as it was before."

"No," the girl demanded, stubbornly, "You have travelled here to save the Queen and her child. Is that not why you and the Lord Paul have come, milady?"

*

"Duffer!" called D.S. Mitchell, cradling his phone.

D.C. Susan Duffy lifted her head out of the file.

"Duffy," she corrected him.

"Whatever," said Mitchell, "There's a Derek Bowman at the desk asking for you?"

"Sugar! I'd forgotten. I'm his shoulder to weep on."

Mitchell put down his phone.

"Shift yourself," he said.

Susan saluted her sergeant rudely and exited the squad room.

As she approached the desk she saw a middle-aged man, receding hair, slightly overweight, schoolboy face, in an expensive suit, reading the posters on the lobby wall.

"Mister Bowman?"

Derek Bowman turned and regarded her soberly.

"I thought it would be a police officer."

"Detective Constable Susan Duffy?"

He was momentarily discomforted and then he grinned.

"I bet you're great undercover."

"I'll take that as a compliment."

The grin vanished and Derek Bowman said, "I thought we'd start where my son died."

Susan nodded agreement.

*

90

On the pavement, Susan looked around for Bowman's car. She was startled and whistled in surprise when brought the large SUV to life with his key ring.

"Wow!" Susan cried, "It's a humvee! Are we going to war?"

"Hummer," Derek Bowman corrected her, "Hummer H1 to be pedantic."

This guy loves this truck. It's the ultimate big boy's toy.

She walked round the SUV.

"It's a four door pickup truck," she rejoiced, "I'm going to ride in a four door pickup truck. *It was the pickup truck that ruined Minnesota.* Tell me it was made in Minnesota!"

"Mishawaka, Indiana."

"Mishawaka, Indiana! I'm going to ride in a four door pickup truck made in Mishawaka, Indiana!"

Derek Bowman laughed at her enthusiasm.

"Maybe, sometime, I'll let you drive."

Susan stopped to look at the bull bars on the front elevation.

"If you hit anybody with this rack you're going to kill them, Mister Bowman. I'm not sure it's legal."

"Call me Derek. Nobody's ever questioned them in Berlin."

"That's where you work?"

"Mostly."

"You drove this all the way from Berlin?"

"It's not the cheapest way to travel."

"But it gets you noticed?"

Susan climbed into the Hummer and strapped herself in. She was surprised how quietly and smoothly the SUV moved away.

*

Derek Bowman parked the Hummer outside 39, Wellington Terrace. Susan Duffy and Bowman exited the SUV. The street was composed of three-storey Victorian houses fronted by gravel drives, well-kept gardens and shaded by mature kerbside trees.

"Thirty nine?" Susan commented, "Your wife lives at thirty nine?"

"Ex-wife. We're barely speaking."

Pity, thought Susan, *coffee and a Wagon Wheel would've been very welcome.*

Derek Bowman and the detective constable walked down the terrace.

"This is where the accident happened," Susan Duffy stated, checking the RTA diagram in her hand.

They stood at approximately the spot where Paul died. The rebuilt garden wall marked where the car involved had ended up.

"Where my son was murdered," Derek Bowman corrected the young detective.

Susan Duffy didn't contradict the bereaved father. Mr. Bowman had informed her inspector that he intended to find the people who murdered his children and kill them. Inspector Starling took the threat seriously enough for W.D.C. Duffy to be allocated as babysitter to Mr. Bowman. *Duff job? Give it to Duffy!*

*

"What am I supposed to do, sir?"

"Keep him out of trouble."

Why does he bother to keep me around? Why not dump me on Traffic or Records? Or does it amuse him to run me around on duff jobs?

Detective Constable Duffy carefully wrote *keep him out of trouble in her notebook* and turned her best information-seeking face upon the inspector.

"How exactly am I supposed to do that, sir?"

Inspector Harold Starling studied the young woman. *Defiant face. Red hair. Legs of a rugby forward.*

"You think this is a duff job? I'm giving it to you because you're a woman?"

Susan Duffy considered for a moment, wrote *yes* in her notebook and replied, "No, sir. I don't think you'd do that. You're a man of integrity."

Oh, Sue! Susan thought, *How can you keep your face straight and lie to him so blatantly?*

The Inspector interrupted her thoughts to say, "Derek Bowman has just lost his son and daughter. He believes the Connollys murdered his children. His son died in a road accident. His daughter died of a massive heart attack. If he's going to "investigate" their deaths. I don't want it to end up with Bowman killing Brian Connolly or vice versa. Do you understand me?"

"Who is this Vice Versa, sir?" asked the Detective Constable, "Is he Italian?"

The inspector glared at Susan.

"Humour him. Keep him out of trouble."

"What about overtime, sir?"

The inspector bit the bullet.

"Keep him out of trouble."

*

An approaching car forced Derek Bowman and the detective constable back onto the pavement where she stood consulting her notes. Susan tried to make up her mind about Derek Bowman.

He doesn't seem a nutter to me. Do I tell him what I know? Or will he think I'm the loony?

"I know you're bored," Derek Bowman said.

Susan Duffy shook her head in denial.

"I'm here to help you."

"No, you're not. You're here to humour me. Your inspector thinks I'm off my head. That I'm inventing a fantasy when really Paul died in a traffic accident. And Amy died of a heart attack."

"What if I said I believed you?"

Derek Bowman laughed sourly.

"As I said, you're here to humour me."

"I've read the statements made by Amy and the driver of the car. It seems to me that."

Derek Bowman interrupted to say, "Your inspector says not to rely on what either thinks they remember. In the trauma of the accident such statements are confused or misleading. Nothing they say can be corroborated."

Susan realised Mr. Bowman was reading from material Inspector Harold Starling had provided for him.

"May I see?" she enquired.

Bowman surrendered the sheets to her. Susan quickly scanned the pages and then tore the document in two and then into four pieces. For an instant, she was tempted to throw the scraps into the air and shout, "Shabby wedding!" But more prudently, she stuffed them into her jacket pocket.

"What're you doing?"

"It's nonsense," said Susan.

"The driver says he saw a child in fancy dress with a catapult."

Susan said, "This is a posh area. Janet and John country. The kids here are indoors by nine. These kids don't throw stones at cars."

Bowman shook his head in denial, but Susan pressed on, "There's no sighting of a child. We've been door to door. All the children in the surrounding roads are accounted for."

Derek Bowman insisted, "But Amy saw something too."

Susan Duffy looked into Derek Bowman's face and recognised the anguish that never goes away. She made her decision. *If I'm wrong he'll create merry hell and I'll be out on my ear. I won't even make Records.*

"Your children were murdered, Mister Bowman," Susan said, "But not by the Connollys. That's not how they function. If you upset Brian Connolly, he'd cut your ears off, but he wouldn't kill your kids."

"But they were murdered," Derek Bowman insisted.

Susan nodded agreement.

"What I'm going to say you'll have to take on trust."

"Say it," said Derek Bowman.

"I know who killed Paul and Amy. I don't know why, but I know they're guilty."

When Bowman tried to interrupt, Susan waved him to silence.

"I saw them in a video."

Derek Bowman looked disappointed and disbelieving.

"A charity shop was broken into and two men stole clothing. A man dressed in Stuart costume and a dwarf in chain mail with a cross bow."

The dissimilar pair stood in silence on the pavement, the man struggling to make sense of what the young woman had said.

Derek Bowman said, "Amy saw a dwarf. In helmet and armour. Your inspector said she'd been traumatized by the accident. Victims often suffer delusions."

Susan shook her head.

"Amy was right. She saw the dwarf. When the driver thought he saw a child in fancy dress he was really looking at the dwarf. But he couldn't believe what he saw."

The man stood silent on the pavement, frustrated and angry.

The bereaved father said, "When she was lying in the road the dwarf came to look at her. That's what my daughter said. Amy heard his footsteps. Saw his face. Asked him to help her."

Susan said, "The dwarf came to see if she was dead. After the car hit her."

Derek Bowman said, "Then why didn't he..." he hesitated and then ploughed on to say, "Why didn't he kill her?"

"He was disturbed. People would come out at the noise of the crash. It was supposed to look like an accident. So the dwarf got into the car and made his escape."

"What car?" demanded Derek Bowman.

Susan Duffy said, "A car came to him. He didn't go to a car. Someone drove the car past Amy, lying in the road and the dwarf got into that car. The driver wore cowboy boots he stole from the charity shop."

The detective constable went to stand where the dwarf, as reported by Amy, first appeared. Derek Bowman followed her uncertainly.

"Do you believe me, sir?" Susan asked.

Mr. Bowman nodded.

The young detective said, "A missile struck the windscreen. The driver was blinded. We're agreed on that?"

The bereaved father nodded.

"Whatever struck the windscreen didn't enter the car."

"No."

"Then it must've glanced off. And from this angle."

"I presume your lot have searched the street?"

Susan Duffy wasn't listening. She was staring into the kerbside tree. Derek Bowman turned to see what she was looking at.

"My God!" cried the young woman, "Oh, my God!"

"What?"

"There it is! There! See?"

High in the tree, deep in the trunk, stood the shaft of the bolt from the crossbow. As Derek Bowman moved towards the tree, the detective cried, "Stay there, I'm quite capable of climbing a tree."

Susan Duffy climbed up to where, ricocheting from the windscreen, the bolt had all but buried itself. She tried hard, but couldn't remove it. The young detective climbed down slowly, her head buzzing with the implications of the find.

Susan Duffy spoke, slowly, incredulously, testing the words aloud, "The dwarf fired a crossbow bolt at the windscreen of the car that killed your son."

Derek Bowman said, "It happened just as Amy said."

Susan laughed aloud. *Duff job? Give it to Duffy! Oh, yeah?*

"Now we have to find the little bugger! And the murderous bastard behind him!"

For a moment Derek Bowman believed the young detective was about to hug him. But the moment passed.

"This video tape," Derek asked, "Where is it? Can I have a look at it?"

TEN

When Joyce Bowman awoke to a familiar voice she prayed the dream would not fade. Amy stood at her bedside.

"Amy, oh, Amy!" her mother cried and reached for her lost daughter, "Oh, my darling!"

"It's alright, Mum," Amy said, holding her mother tightly, "I'm here."

Joyce Bowman began to weep, clutching her daughter, feeling the warmth, the solidity of her body.

"Please, don't let me wake up!"

Amy wiped her mother's eyes, smiling, "Hush, Mum. We're here. Really here."

From Amy's embrace Joyce glimpsed Paul, hanging back at the bedroom door as he always did: *Come here you*, his mother would say to the boy-child at the bed foot, *I've lots of hugs. Don't you play second fiddle with me. Come here. I'll play a tune on you.*

"Play a tune on me," said Paul and laughed, coming to embrace his mother.

"Oh, Paul!" cried Joyce, "Is it really you?"

"Who else," Paul retorted, "would make his Mother cry at the sight of him?"

Joyce Bowman laughed, wiped her tears and said, "I don't understand. If it's not a dream."

Amy said, "How can we explain what's inexplicable, Mum?"

"Time travel is something like falling off a cliff," said Paul, "and never hitting the rocks."

"Time travel? I can't believe I'm not dreaming. This is a dream."

"You're not dreaming," assured Amy, "We have a purpose in being here."

Paul said, "We have a mission to complete."

"Don't question what's happening," Amy suggested, "Accept what you see to be true."

"What mission?" Joyce Bowman questioned the teenagers.

How can I believe what is not possible?

"A terrible wrong has been done," said Paul, "and we have been chosen to put it right."

"But why you? Why would anyone choose you?"

Please, God, don't let this dream end. Don't take them away from me again.

"It has to do with twins, our birth date, and a certain place at a certain time."

"Jedburgh. The Jethart House," Amy added, "Remember? We went on field trip?"

"But you're dead," lamented their mother, overwhelmed by the truth of two funerals, "I know you are. That's the truth of it, isn't it? Tell me. Or else I shall go mad."

The twins exchanged glances and Amy took her mother's hand.

"There is a price to pay to cross time's boundaries."

Paul said, "The science-fiction writers have got it wrong. There are no free rides. The price is death."

"Then you're dead!" cried Joyce, "Nothing can change that."

The anguish in her breast was overwhelming.

"But we're here now, Mum," Amy persisted, "Isn't that enough? For us to be together now? For whatever time we have?"

The painful silence was broken by Joyce Bowman who questioned, "You said Jedburgh? The Field Trip?"

"It's all to do with Mary, Queen of Scots and the Jethart House," said Paul.

"I read the guide book," their mother agreed, "The Queen travelled to Jedburgh to hold an Assize Court, but secretly to see her lover the Earl Bothwell."

"Wrong!" said Amy, "Mary didn't ride to Jedburgh to hold an assize court. Nor did she ride to Hermitage to see Bothwell. It's all lies. She was escaping to England. Riding to Newcastle. Escaping from her husband, Henry Darnley. And Bothwell tried to take her prisoner."

"It's one of history's great lies," Paul declared.

"Slow down," said Joyce Bowman, "Your mother's not too bright."

I'm behaving as if this were real. As if they've brought home an essay question from school.

"Mary was next in line to the English throne," Amy explained, "She didn't want her baby, James, to be born in Edinburgh. She wanted him born in England. So she fled from Edinburgh, narrowly escaped capture at Hermitage Castle and ended up besieged in Jedburgh by James Hepburn, Earl of Bothwell."

"We desperately need your help, Mum," Paul pleaded, "There's no one else can help us."

Joyce Bowman struggled to understand.

An essay question for A Level History. If Henry the Eighth had had eight wives would that be a world record? Discuss.

"You're talking as if the siege was going on now."

"Yes, it is. Bothwell won't let anyone in or out of the House."

"Then how can I help you?"

I'll buy some decent paper for you tomorrow. Make a decent job of it. And a new ink cartridge for the printer. Just in case. You're joking! The essay has to be handwritten!

"The baby isn't born yet."

"There's a problem?"

"He's in the breach position, Mum."

I know the answer to this one.

"Surely there's a midwife? An experienced midwife can cope with that. She must manipulate the child."

"Mum, please, don't be angry," Paul confessed, "Mary's here. In Amy's room."

*

Derek Bowman asked, "You were with my wife the night my daughter Amy was abducted?"

David Griffiths nodded. D.C. Susan Duffy noted he couldn't keep still. His left leg drummed the floor incessantly.

He looks like the walking dead, thought Susan. *Depression. Anxiety attacks. Sleeplessness. Weeping for little or no cause.*

From the kitchen they heard the voices of Isobel Griffiths and the children. Then the front door closed and there was silence.

"You've been off sick since that night," Susan Duffy suggested.

David Griffiths nodded.

Derek Bowman thought, *this little rat's on the edge of a breakdown.* He felt a sudden surge of anger, but he controlled himself to say, "We'd like to learn what made you behave as you did."

David Griffiths said, "I don't want to talk about it."

"You might help us understand why the young people died," Susan Duffy suggested.

Derek Bowman regarded the quivering man with contempt, but said, as gently as he could contrive, "We need your help, David. Please?"

The young man reacted violently, crying out, "For God's case, I'm ill! Can't you see? I'm ill!"

"You'd feel better if you got it off your chest," Derek Bowman said, brusquely, fighting the urge to take the sad creature by the throat. Susan Duffy reading his body language said, "David, why won't you help us?"

David Griffiths stood up, trembling.

"I want you to leave."

He called out, "Isobel!"

Susan Duffy said, "Your wife's gone out. She took the children with her."

David Griffiths sat down.

"Why don't you just leave me in peace? There's nothing I can tell you."

Derek Bowman persisted, "David, you're our only chance of tracking down the people who killed my children."

The young man shook his head, his left leg drumming faster and faster.

When Derek moved, Susan Duffy gestured for him to sit down, saying, "David, you're a trained policeman."

"I've put in my papers."

"What's been happening is real, David. Buried in a tree in Wellington Terrace is a crossbow bolt. I've seen it. The dwarf is real."

The fear in David Griffiths' eyes was electric. He looked as if he were about to weep. *He's met the dwarf,* thought Derek Bowman, *He's scared witless.* When he looked to Susan Duffy he saw she knew too.

"I don't know any dwarf."

"The dwarf in the mail coat? With the helmet? The crossbow?" Susan Duffy suggested.

"I just want to be left alone," David Griffiths pleaded.

Derek Bowman lost his temper and shouted, "Well, you're bloody well not going to be," and the young man began to weep, rocking in his chair. Susan Duffy rose to put a comforting arm about his shoulders. She gave Derek Bowman a warning glance that he ignored.

"For God's sake," Derek Bowman shouted, "what've you got to weep about?"

"I can't sleep!" David Griffiths wailed, "I mustn't sleep!"

"Pull yourself together, man!" Derek Bowman shouted, "You disgust me!"

David Griffiths wept like a child, wailing his grief. "I can't sleep!"

The distraught father towered over the young man, fists clenched.

"Calm down, Mister Bowman," Susan suggested, "We're getting nowhere. Let me talk to him."

Reluctantly, Derek Bowman agreed. Susan Duffy comforted the distraught Griffiths.

"I wish I was dead."

"No you don't. Think of your wife and children. They need you."

"If I had any guts I'd top myself. Only I'm yellow through and through."

With a flash of intuition the young woman said, "That's not cowardice, David."

She silenced Bowman's contemptuous anger: "It certainly sounds like it," with a gesture.

"That's not cowardice. That's you fighting back. Your true self doesn't want to die. But somebody wants you to. You're a victim too. Somehow these people have got to you. I don't know how. Drugs? Hypnotism? You've got to help us find them, David. Help us stop them."

Her approach seemed to comfort, to strengthen the young man.

"So tell us, please. Whatever you know. Whatever you can remember."

They sat in a long, painful silence. Susan Duffy could sense Derek Bowman's irritation and signalled him to patience.

"I remember," David Griffiths said.

My God, thought Susan, *he's absolutely terrified.*

"Go on," she said gently.

"Promise you won't tell anyone?"

"I promise," Susan Duffy said and Derek Bowman snorted his impatience.

"Spit it out for God's sake!" Derek Bowman snarled.

"Mister Bowman, unless you can control yourself, I will ask you to leave."

The silence seemed endless and then David Griffiths confessed, "When I came on duty. I had this terrible urge. To kill the girl. Amy. I wanted to kill her. I really wanted to."

"Why would you want to do that?"

"There was this voice in my head."

Derek Bowman snorted his disbelief.

"Go on," invited Susan Duffy.

"I answered the telephone. I think I answered the telephone. And He said..."

"He? What's his name?"

"I don't know."

"Can you can remember what he said!"

The young man hesitated, and then, "He said. Take the woman out of the house and I will come."

"You bastard!" cried Derek Bowman, "You betrayed them! You let that devil into the house!"

Susan Duffy said, "Mister Bowman, I'm conducting this interrogation. If you continue to interrupt, I will insist you leave."

"The inspector was telling me to bring Missis Bowman to the station and He was talking at the same time."

David Griffiths began to weep. Derek Bowman scowled his frustration as the detective signalled him to be silent. When David Griffiths was able to continue, Susan, guided by intuition, said, "You've met this man, haven't you? Not only talked with him on the phone. You've met him. To control you like this you had to meet him. Tell me where."

"I don't remember."

"Yes, you do. Think hard. You do remember."

The clock on the sitting room mantelpiece chimed softly. As the chimes died away David Griffiths said, in an uncertain voice, "There's a house in Convent Passage."

"Number?"

The young man shook his head.

"I don't know."

"Yes, you do."

"Forty. Seven. On the third floor. There's a room."

"Has it a number?"

"The blue door."

"And you met him there?"

"I opened the door and went in."

"Was he surprised to see you?"

The young man shook his head.

"Was he alone?"

"The dwarf was with him. And a woman."

"Can you remember anything he said?"

"He said, 'Here comes yet one other seeking the path to the Jethart House.'"

The policewoman and Derek Bowman exchanged glances.

"Did he tell you his name?"

David Griffiths hesitated for an eternity.

"James Hepburn. Earl of Bothwell."

Susan Duffy silenced Bowman's incredulity.

"Then the dwarf hurt me," said the young man, "When I sleep, he hurts me again. I wish I was dead."

David Griffiths began to weep as if he would never stop.

*

Susan Duffy shut her eyes while Derek Bowman squeezed the Hummer into the smallest parking space on Earth in Convent Passage.

Reading her face, Derek said, "Oh ye of little faith!"

"I hope you can get it out again."

They walked along the terrace to number forty-seven, mounted the steps and stopped.

"What now?"

As if in answer to unspoken prayer a young woman came out from the front door and Susan caught the door before it closed.

"Excuse me," said the young woman, "I don't think you live here?"

Susan flashed her warrant card.

"A blue door? Top floor?"

The young woman shook her head.

"Sorry! I think all our doors are black?"

They climbed the stairs together, checking doors on the first floor and then ascended to the second floor. There were two black doors and one blue door. Susan was about to knock when she realised there was no door furniture. She turned the handle and the blue door opened.

It was a caretaker's cupboard equipped with brooms, mops, brushes and cleaning equipment. As Susan turned to Derek Bowman a voice behind them asked, "Can I help you?"

A small man with a big moustache, dressed in a khaki overall, had followed them up the stairs. Susan flashed her warrant card and the caretaker said, "You've come about the bleach, have you? 'bout time! Three bottles gone in a week! And a mop head! Expect you'll want to question all the tenants, but I put my money on Bradley-Alsopp in 47D. What sort of a name is that? Good cop, bad cop, you'll soon gerrim to cough!"

*

"This is Mary?" said Doctor Bowman, incredulously, "Mary, Queen of Scots?"

Even as she spoke the eyelids of the woman lying on the bed in the bloodstained nightdress flickered as she struggled to speak and failed.

"I need my bag," said the doctor.

"I'll get it," Amy decided and exited.

Joyce Bowman said, "I don't understand what's happening. But I'm going to act as if I did."

Paul grinned and said, "You're a star, Ma!"

When Amy returned her mother examined the patient while the teenagers fretted in silence.

"Well, Mum?"

Joyce Bowman slowly coiled the stethoscope and returned it to her medical bag.

"There's nothing I can do."

"But, Mum!"

"Ring for an ambulance."

Paul said, "We can't do that."

"She needs a hospital now if there's to be any chance of saving her!"

"No," insisted Amy, "she can't go to hospital."

"Then she'll die."

"She can't go to hospital," Paul said, "That's not possible."

"Believe me, Mum," said Amy, "we can't intrude any further. It must be a natural birth."

"If we involve twentieth century technology," Paul declared, "the consequences will be catastrophic."

"How can you possibly know this?"

"Trust me, Mum. We know," Amy pleaded, "This far and no further."

"Do what you can, Mum," Paul added, "Mary and her baby either live or die here."

Doctor Bowman looked down on the woman, moaning in pain, struggling to breathe.

"She can't give birth."

"But you must save the baby," cried Amy.

The doctor shook her head.

"I will try to save the mother," Doctor Bowman decided, "But the baby is either dead or dying."

"That can't be!" Paul declared, "This baby has a great destiny ahead of him."

The doctor smiled wryly, "Paul, I don't know whether I'm dreaming. Or whether this nightmare is real."

Paul embraced his mother. She felt the solid warmth of him. Amy took her hand and she struggled not to weep, remembering two coffins.

"I don't understand," Joyce Bowman said sadly.

Amy said, "This baby is to be a king. He's going to unite the two kingdoms. James the First of England. James the Sixth of Scotland."

"Then there must be other babies," Doctor Bowman assured her daughter.

"But that's why we've crossed over," cried Amy in anguish, "To save them. Mary and her baby."

"Mum," Paul urged, "please, please help us! Or everything will go wrong. We died for nothing."

"Oh, darlings," said Joyce Bowman, "It's too late. The heartbeat is failing. The baby is dying."

ELEVEN

The dwarf peered in through the grating and the creature that had been Detective Constable David Griffiths whimpered aloud.

"Please, God, dear God, don't let him come in! Don't let him come in! Don't let him hurt me again!"

His bladder betrayed him when the lock grated and the heavy door began to creak open. Crouching naked in the corner, urine dribbling from his knees, David began to scream when the dwarf came into the dungeon. Cymian struck him on the head with the handle of his dagger, snarling, "Quit thy squeal, pig, or I'll take thy tongue! My master has a question for you."

David became aware another man stood beside the dwarf. When he looked up, dazed by the light from the doorway he knew he was looking at his death. The face that smiled down at him displayed no kindness.

"I trust you are comfortable in our care?" Bothwell enquired.

David nodded abjectly.

"The food, wines, service are all of the best? You have the finest duck-down and bed linen?"

The wretched man nodded again. Cymian sniggered.

"If you were to have a complaint, however trivial, you shall have the pleasure of castrating the offender."

The dwarf said, "Say thanks be, to his Lordship."

"Thanks be to your Lordship," David Griffiths mumbled through torn gums that bled still.

"Similarly, I shall feel free to remove your manhood should you fail to answer my questions. And feed it to you with a dish of greens."

Cymian laughed and capered with delight. David Griffiths whimpered.

"Tell me about this woman. This 'police' woman. Susan Duffy."

Cymian kicked his prisoner into speech.

"What do you want to know?"

"She has household? Husband, children?"

David Griffiths shook his head.

"Mother? Father?"

"I don't know. We didn't work the same shifts."

In the silence David Griffiths whimpered aloud.

"Tell me what she fears."

"What she fears?"

"You are not deaf."

The dwarf struck David Griffiths across the face. His nose began to bleed again.

"What does this woman fear most? Fire? Water? Falling?"

"I don't know."

The terrified face was a clown mask of blood.

"What does she fear? With what may I prise her open?"

*

The doctor said, "What time did you last look in on Mister Griffiths?"

"Seven thirty. It's logged on the sheet."

"Any change in his behaviour?"

"No, sir. He hides in a corner. Under the bed. He screams if I go near him."

"Who deals with his medication?"

"Sharon. Only one gets near him. Griffiths thinks she's his wife. Calls her Isobel. He'll eat if she sits with him."

"And when you checked him at?"

"Eight ten. He was lying on the floor. Thought he was asleep."

"But he wasn't?"

"Mister Griffiths had opened up his mattress. He stuffed his throat, mouth, nose tight with the kapok. He died choking on his own vomit."

*

Joyce Bowman straightened up from her examination.

"It's a footling breach. Heart beat irregular. I don't understand it."

Paul asked, "What does that mean? Footling breach?"

Amy sat beside the bed, held Mary's hand and talked to her soothingly in a whisper.

"In a word the baby's put its foot in it. Both feet."

"The arms," Paul said, slowly, "that means."

Amy pleaded, "You must turn him round, Mum!"

"The baby is already engaged," said her mother, puzzled, "and I don't understand the heartbeat. Sometimes..." she stopped, "We have the ingredients of tragedy here."

"Please, Mum," Amy begged, "make a miracle."

"The only thing I can do."

"Then do it," Amy interrupted, "If there's a chance of life. For Mary. The baby. Do it, please."

"I'm going to deliver the baby. It's not going to be pleasant. If the mother withstands the trauma then there's a chance she'll live. The baby has little prospect of survival. The mother has to be my priority. Are we agreed?"

The teenagers' agonised silence heralded their acquiescence. While Amy and Paul held Mary, stroked her brow and held her lovingly, Doctor Bowman firmly, powerfully, withdrew the baby. Mary screamed in her agony, twisted, mumbled, bit her lip until the blood ran down her chin and grasped Paul's hand vice-tight. She screamed for mercy as the baby was drawn onto the bed.

"I'm sorry," Doctor Bowman decided. "The baby is dead. There's no more I can do."

"That can't be!" Amy cried, "That's not what's meant to happen!"

Paul stood bewildered.

"But he is to be a king!"

Amy wept by the bed.

Dr. Bowman said, quietly, "No king. This child was a girl."

"A girl?" Paul questioned, "That's wrong! Mary had a boy. James!"

The twins faced each other in despair.

"If James isn't born that changes everything."

Mary stirred and cried out in a convulsion of pain. Her body struggled with a further contraction.

Amy asked, "What's happening? Is she dying?"

She looked to her brother in dismay.

Doctor Bowman clapped her hands.

"Of course! How stupid of me! Twins!" she cried, "The heart beat! There's another baby!"

The twins shared amazement and delight.

"Now," Amy declared, "Now I understand about the Gemini."

*

"Has anyone seen Timothy?" D.C. Susan Duffy called out to the squad room, "The cadet? John Timothy? Looks like Bugs Bunny?"

There was no response.

"No one at all?"

Susan gave up, grabbed her bag and headed for the stairs. Waiting for the lift, which Susan never used, was W.P.C. Melanie McLennon with an armful of files.

"Hi, Mel! I don't suppose you've seen our cadet? John Timothy?"

The lift door opened as Melanie said, "Not since I gave him your info on the Morris Traveller."

The lift door closed as she said, "How did that work out?"

Susan flew down the stairs faster than a drunken skier.

When the lift door opened, Melanie almost dropped her burden of files.

"Wow! What did I say?"

"You said how did that work out. How did what work out?"

"About the Morris Traveller."

"What about the Morris Traveller?"

Susan helped Melanie adjust her stack of files.

Melanie said, patiently, "You asked me to find out about a Morris Traveller."

He didn't tell me. I'll kill the twerp when I catch up with him.

"I've forgotten. Tell me again."

Melanie eyed the young detective with some reproach.

"You wanted to know the whereabouts of a certain Morris Traveller. No action needed. You have something going."

"So?"

"Well, when traffic found the car it was parked at the Old Sally."

Susan pondered this information.

"When did you tell the cadet?"

Melanie shrugged.

"Thursday? Friday?"

Susan said, "Thanks, Mel. I owe you one."

"No bother," said Melanie, and turning away, "Did you slide down the banister?"

Susan laughed.

"Parachute?"

At the desk Susan asked for and wrote into her notebook John Timothy's address. On the pavement, dialling Derek Bowman's mobile number she said aloud, "I need a few words with that young man."

*

Derek Bowman parked the Hummer below the block of flats.

"I'll bet you even money the lift isn't working."

On the landing, Susan said, "Derek, let me do the talking. You shouldn't even be with me."

Derek Bowman looked hurt.

"How can you keep me out of trouble if I'm not with you?"

Susan rang the bell.

"Derek, please, keep your gob zipped."

A pleasant, middle-aged woman, whom Susan immediately knew was John Timothy's mother, opened the door.

"Mrs. Timothy? Detective Constable Susan Duffy?"

Susan made no attempt to introduce Derek Bowman who smiled and nodded.

"Please, come in!" said Mrs. Timothy, "I feel I know you, Susan. John has talked about you often. You're his hero."

An embarrassed detective constable stepped into the hallway of the flat. Derek Bowman followed somewhat diffidently.

"I wonder if I might have a word with John?"

"Oh, I'm sorry," said Mrs. Timothy, "He's not here."

The young detective and Derek Bowman followed John's mother into a neatly furnished sitting room.

"Please do sit down. I've just put the kettle on."

"I'm sorry," Susan apologised, "We're rather short of time. Do you know where John is?"

His mother looked puzzled.

"When did you last see him?" Susan said, struggling to sound casual and unconcerned when instinct was screaming something terrible had happened.

"Thursday?" said his mother, "He said he was on an important job. Couldn't talk about it. It would be a real biggie."

Missis Timothy looked hopefully to Susan.

D.C. Duffy lied, "It's a bit hush-hush."

The cadet's mother relaxed and Susan Duffy hated herself.

To her surprise, Derek Bowman spoke.

"What we really came for, Missis Timothy, is a video tape John may have."

Mrs. Timothy interrupted to say, "Oh, yes! I know what you mean. I think it's still in his TV."

She vanished as Susan glared at Derek Bowman and returned with the familiar tape.

"He was very excited. He said, Mum, always see the movie right through to the credits. Or you won't get the whole picture. I don't know what he meant, but I'm sure you do."

She smiled and surrendered the tape.

*

Sitting in the Hummer, Susan said, "I lied to that dear woman. I have no idea where John Timothy is. But I'm very afraid for him."

Derek Bowman started the engine.

"Let's go see this movie through to the credits."

The only machine that would play videotape at the Marriott was a dusty machine in the Head Chef's office. Susan and Derek Bowman sat eating chicken sandwiches to watch the video through to the end.

*

On first sight the child had no face and Amy cried out her alarm. Doctor Bowman wiped away the caul and upended the child to strike his tiny buttocks smartly. His first cry released the tension and the Bowmans laughed aloud. Doctor Bowman clamped the cord and cut the child free.

Paul said, voice trembling, "You do realise, Mum? You've just belted the past and future king of Scotland and England?"

Doctor Bowman said, "And what of his sister? Poor nameless child."

Paul and Amy were sobered by this thought.

"I think," said their mother, "That she will sleep as well under the beech tree in our garden as anywhere else."

On this they were agreed.

Mary, barely conscious, struggled to speak.

"Bebe? Vive-t'il?"

"Your son, madam."

Doctor Bowman presented the child within her vision. The Queen visibly relaxed.

"Dieu soit loue," she whispered, smiling.

Joyce Bowman said admiringly, "Madam, you are one tough cookie!"

Mary smiled, not comprehending, but understanding the intention and lay back, closing her eyes.

"Is he all right, Mum?" asked Amy as her mother examined the baby.

"He's fine."

"Will the Queen live?"

"She's survived the births. That's the first hurdle. If she has proper care. If she's not moved."

"She can stay here," Amy said, "until."

Paul interrupted to say, "Until the matter is resolved."

"What matter?" asked his mother, but was ignored.

*

There was no Morris Traveller parked at the Old Sally. Susan and Derek Bowman climbed out of the Hummer.

"You didn't really expect it to be still here?" asked Derek Bowman, "If it was ever here."

Susan shook her head, walking the gutter along the old City Wall. "Nothing is that easy."

Derek ran his hands over the stonework of the old sally gate.

"There was once a gate here. Neat patching, but you can still see the gate."

Susan stopped.

"The Traveller was here."

Derek came to join the young detective who was kneeling to examine the tyre mark on the drying mud in the gutter.

"Wha'd'y'think?"

"Five twenty fourteen," said Derek.

"How do'y'know that?"

"Twenty five years in the trade? 'bout right for a car of that age."

"Then if the Traveller was here," Susan decided, "Then Timothy was here."

They walked the pavement along the old wall, but before the old sally

Gate, Derek Bowman stopped.

"Could these be blood stains?"

Derek Bowman brought the First Aid case from the Hummer and the detective constable scraped fragments of the suspicious stains onto lint and sealed it into a plastic bag.

While they were on their knees a shadow fell over them. Even before she looked up, Susan could smell the man's stink. The alkie stood, hands trembling and stepped back when the pair rose to confront him.

"Good afternoon, sir," the detective constable said, "Have you ever seen a Morris Traveller parked here?"

The alkie smirked to say, "That'd be telling."

"Do'y'know what a Traveller looks like?" asked Derek Bowman.

"Wha'd'y'take me for?"

Derek opened his mouth and then changed his mind.

Susan suggested, "Someone who would do their civic duty and help the police?"

The alkie was triumphant.

"I thought ye was. Ye have the face forrit."

"I'll take that as a compliment," said Susan.

Derek Bowman asked, "D'y'spend a lot of time here?"

"I might do."

Derek Bowman said, "Was there a Morris Traveller parked here recently?"

"There might be."

Susan said, "Well, there isn't now."

"They've been and gone," declared the alkie.

Keeping patience, Susan suggested, "Why don't you tell us what you saw?

The alkie hitched his trousers, winked at the young woman, and said, "What's in it for me?"

Before Susan could reply Derek Bowman said, "Don't go away," and walked towards the Hummer.

"What does ya mannie think about ye doing this?" enquired the alkie.

"I don't have a mannie," said Susan shortly.

"Thought not," the alkie smiled.

Derek Bowman returned with a whisky bottle. He waved it before the alkie's faded blue eyes.

"You tell us what happened here. And maybe I'll give you a sup."

Susan objected, "You can't do that, Derek!"

"You can't, but I can."

With his eyes on the bottle, the alkie said, "There's no a lot to tell. He wasnie a proper pollis. Just a lad. He went to speak to them and the wee man stuck him twice with his knife and killed him."

Susan gasped and suddenly felt sick.

Derek Bowman said, "Who's them?"

Susan struggled not to weep. Her legs almost failed her and she put a hand to Derek Bowman's shoulder.

The alkie said, "The big man. And the wee man."

Derek Bowman asked, "The big man? Got a beard? Leather jacket, trousers?"

"That's the yin," the alkie agreed.

Susan said, "They killed the police cadet?"

"Aye. The wee man stuck him twice."

Susan said, "Then they put the cadet in the Traveller?"

The alkie shook his head.

"That's the queer thing. They dragged him through the wall."

The alkie indicated the wall beside them.

Derek Bowman said, "Through the wall? Not over the wall? Through the wall?"

"Aye. They took an arm each and walked through the wall, dragging the lad behind them."

Susan said, "They vanished through the wall?"

The alkie said, "Are yis deef? I cannae keep saying it. They walked through the wall."

Susan and Derek stared at the old stone city wall.

"You're a liar!" decided Susan.

The alkie was indignant.

"Why should I lie? If I wanted to lie I wad say they dumped the poor lad in the car. But they didn't. They walked through that stone wall dragging the lad's body like it was nowt."

"Then what happened?"

"I had me a wee snooze and when I woke up the car was gone."

"You haven't seen them since?"

The alkie shook his head.

"Ye promised me a drink."

Derek Bowman produced a cardboard coffee cup and filled it from the bottle. The alkie seized it from his hand and drank half in one swallow.

"Ah, but you're a real gentleman, sir, God bless yi!"

In the Hummer they sat in a silence that neither was keen to break. Finally Susan said, "Is there anything left in that bottle?"

Derek Bowman produced the whisky and gave it to the detective constable. Susan drank from the bottle and then drank again. Derek Bowman took the bottle from her as she raised it to her mouth yet again.

He asked, "Do you think he's telling the truth?"

Susan nodded.

"Yes."

"Then we're dealing with serial killers."

"No," Susan decided, "The Earl of Bothwell and his dwarf are behaving just as they would in their own time."

"I don't follow. What own time?""

"This is not a singular universe. Bothwell and the dwarf have access to our time through antique sites. The Castle car park."

"Car park?"

"Was the bailey of the motte and bailey castle. Convent Passage. The ancient Carmelite Convent. And the old sally gate."

Derek Bowman pondered on the proposition.

"Are you seriously suggesting this Bothwell travelled through time? To kill people?"

"I don't know why yet, but this nightmare started when your children went on a school trip to the Jethart House at Jedburgh. When they returned this creature Bothwell started killing innocent people."

Derek Bowman said, "Travelling through time to kill them for what?"

Susan said, "Poor David Griffiths told us what Bothwell said to him."

The young policewoman checked her notebook and recited, "Here comes yet one other seeking the path to the Jethart House."

"You're asking me to believe those bastards travelled from the past to kill my children because they'd been to this damned House?"

Susan said, "I don't want to believe in time travel. But the two men in that video weren't going to a fancy dress party. I believe Bothwell and his dwarf killed your children. A nurse and a teacher. David Griffiths. And now John Timothy. Anyone who stumbles on to the path to the Jethart House."

Derek Bowman said, "Somebody must've taught this madman, Bothwell, the rudiments of driving."

"So?"

"Somewhere there's an antique car missing, nobody's missed yet. And a dead body, nobody's discovered yet. Probably a woman."

"Why d'y'say a woman?"

"A woman could be flattered into showing this man how to drive. I think some women would find him attractive."

Susan pondered this theory.

"Why not a man?"

"I think a man would question why a man of his age didn't know the basics. But a woman is looking at this big, attractive man. She mistakes his interest in her car for interest in herself."

"I hope you're wrong."

*

It had taken the courier, even with the aid of his satnav, a tedious hour to find the lane. In Jedburgh, everyone had shaken his or her head at Binny Lane. Even as he drove cautiously from the Edinburgh road up the rutted, green-roofed lane he was doubtful of finding the house. When the lane turned into the farmyard that was no longer a farmyard and the farmhouse that was no longer a farmhouse he breathed a sigh of relief.

He climbed out of his van, collected the package and with his electronic pad in hand went to pull the bell beside the sun-blistered door. The bell jangled loudly inside the house. No one answered the door. The courier repeatedly pulled the bell. No one came to answer his summons. Checking his watch, he stepped back from the house. The sagging garage doors stood open. The garage was empty.

The courier completed his circuit of the house, finding the kitchen door locked. No one answered his repeated knocking. Returning to the front door he made up his mind. Checking the details, he scribbled a hieroglyphic that might have been McKenzie on his pad, added time and date, placed the package safely inside the porch and returned to his van. He reversed the van and dived back into the green pool of the lane. With a little luck he'd be home in time for Eastenders.

However, he was mistaken in thinking the elderly McKenzie sisters, Polly and Muriel, were not at home. Polly, with her throat cut from ear to ear, lay dead on the sitting room floor amidst the wreckage of Mother's best blue and white bone china tea service. Muriel had escaped so far as to reach her bedroom where she had been repeatedly stabbed and bled to death on a valuable antique counterpane.

*

"John Timothy was a good kid," said Susan Duffy, "He would've made a good copper. A good detective. I swear, I'm going to find this Bothwell and his loathsome dwarf."

"You think you can bring these sixteenth century bastards to court?" questioned Derek Bowman sceptically.

"If I can't," decided Detective Constable Duffy, "Then I'll kill them."

The alkie wandered past the Hummer and waved at them.

"It began in Jedburgh," said Susan, "In a house where Mary, Queen of Scots once stayed."

Susan paused and then said, "Will you come with me to Jedburgh?"

*

Doctor Bowman wrapped the past and future king of England and Scotland, despite his protests, in a towel printed Property of N.Y.P.D.

Paul kissed his mother.

"You're a miracle worker, Mum. I knew you could do it. No one else could've pulled it off."

"Mary's safe," Amy said to her brother, "They're both safe. Then we must go."

"Go? Go where?" their mother questioned.

"We must return to the Jethart House and finish what we've begun."

"No, you mustn't," Joyce Bowman pleaded, "You must stay here."

"We have no choice, Mum," Amy said sadly, "You must have faith. You must trust us."

The Queen tried to sit up and when Doctor Bowman turned from the bed, Paul and Amy were gone. As a lamp is darkened. Extinguished.

TWELVE

"I didn't know this was here," Paul said, as he climbed out onto the fighting platform that had been built about the chimneystack on the roof of the House. A bowman's friendly hand pulled him to his feet.

"We have to keep these villains under observation," commented John Traquair.

"You said something interesting?" Paul questioned.

"Strange certainly," said John Traquair, "Interesting? Perhaps."

Paul joined the captain by the chimneystack.

"I thought they were preparing a weapon, but it isn't. It's a scaffold."

Paul looked to the farther bank of the Jedwater.

"Its purpose is to chill our blood. But the man they're hanging is already dead."

Rising on the hangman's rope, Paul saw the limp figure of a man. What suddenly chilled his blood was the fact the corpse wore trousers. His clothing seemed familiar.

Paul, shocked, turned to John to say, "That man is from another time."

"Surely not, lord!"

"He's wearing a uniform. I would guess a police officer?"

"Why would they do this?" Traquair queried.

Paul shook his head.

"I've no idea."

The corpse now hung clearly visible from every window in the House.

"They've cut off his hands," said Traquair.

Paul saw beyond the cuffs there were no hands. He struggled to cope with the shock of this further atrocity.

"Why would they do that?"

"A thief? I doubt so," Traquair said, "I believe this man was meddling in matters beyond his ken. This message is for you, lord."

"Then the message is too late."

Paul turned to the bowman.

"Can you reach that hangman from here?"

"No, lord."

John Traquair said, "May be we can. With Wilhemina."

The bowman shared a smile with Traquair.

"Come," said Traquair and a puzzled Paul followed him round the chimneystack.

Paul gasped. Mounted on an iron stand was the biggest crossbow he had ever seen.

"Wilhemina, lord," said the bowman, grinning and began to wind the ratchet below the monstrous bow.

Paul realised the giant crossbow was an antique; dragged out from a cellar of the House and refurbished to serve again.

"We intend them to keep their distance," said Traquair as he selected a monstrous dart, straightened the flights and placed the bolt on the shaft.

Paul, looking to the royal standard streaming in the breeze, suggested, "You'll need to aim high, reckon the trajectory," and stopped.

Traquair and his bowman were looking at Paul.

"Sorry," said Paul, "Grandmother and eggs."

The bowman settled to his task, judging wind and distance, flight and velocity.

Then he looked to Traquair who nodded. The bowman released the trigger and the bolt soared into the blue.

The man standing next to the hangman fell down and everyone else ran for their lives. The bowman cursed.

Traquair said, "We have answered them, lord," and clapped his bowman on the shoulder.

*

"Would you like to swap a prawn mayonnaise for a smoked salmon and cucumber?" Derek Bowman asked.

Susan Duffy considered the offer carefully, sipping her cola.

"Why would you do that?"

Derek Bowman sighed his exasperation.

"Do you realise how often you answer a question with a question?"

"Is it a rubbish sandwich?"

"Is it becos you is police? You never answer questions?"

Susan Duffy laughed.

"I've never had smoked salmon."

"It's delicious. Try it!"

They exchanged sandwiches.

"Thank you," said Susan.

"This prawn sandwich is very acceptable," Derek Bowman decided.

They ate in silence until Susan Duffy said, "I think I like smoked salmon."

"It's raw fish," said Derek, "But it's been smoked."

"Now you tell me!"

They were sitting in the Hummer parked on the brow of Carter Bar, eating an improvised lunch from a supermarket in Ponteland, gazing out at the Cheviot Hills and the long winding road down into Scotland. The caution that had marked their first acquaintance had long since evaporated. The improbable trail of "evidence" they were following had brought them closer together.

"Your boss okay with this?" Derek asked, "Scooting off to Jedburgh?"

Susan finished her cola and returned the rubbish wrappings to the carrier bag.

"Haven't told him," she said, "Thought better not."

"Why?"

"He'd doubt my sanity."

Derek Bowman laughed.

"My excuse," Susan offered, "is I was told to keep you out of trouble. So if I go to Jedburgh, I guess you go too."

Derek laughed.

They ate in silence until Derek said, "I only spoke to David Griffiths once before," he hesitated and continued, "but he seemed a sensible, level-headed young man."

"He was a dedicated policeman," Susan assured him, "Well respected.

Something horrendous happened to him when he stepped into that cupboard in Convent Passage."

Susan waited out the silence and then suggested, "Do you believe in life after death? Ghosts? That sort of thing?"

Derek Bowman said, "I've never given it much thought."

Susan said, "A couple of years back I was staying with Jen, an old friend, in a stable block she and her husband'd converted. It was late and we were sitting by the fire in the main room. The children long gone to bed. Rob, her husband said goodnight and went to bed, leaving us for a girly chat. So he said."

"An article for Country Life?" interrupted Derek Bowman, "Complete with photos of the spaniels?"

Susan declared continued, "They'd kept some of the features of the old stables. Like the iron spiral staircase that came down from what had been the upper tackle and feed store into the main living room. Jen, Rob, the children and I were the only people in the house. Suddenly there was a breath of cold air as if a door had opened. A young man and a young woman came down the stairs, the man in shirt, breeches and boots, the girl in floor-length brown dress, pinafore and bonnet."

"You mean ghosts?"

"As solid as you or me. But there was no clatter of boots on the iron staircase."

Derek Bowman regarded Susan with some scepticism.

"I don't believe in ghosts."

"Everybody else clattered up and down that staircase. Particularly the children."

"You'd been drinking?"

"No!"

"I'll believe you. Go on!"

"They stopped and stared at us. Jen didn't say a word, but I nodded at them. Then they walked through the wall where once there'd been a door into the stable yard."

Derek was about to speak, but Susan held up a hand.

"Jen said, 'Did you see them?' I said, 'They saw us!'"

Derek couldn't restrain himself.

"You are telling me the truth, aren't you?"

Susan said, "I swear."

Derek nodded for her to continue.

"Jen said, 'We often see the old couple in the garden. And there's a dog that follows Jack around.' I asked why didn't they do something? Exorcism, perhaps? Jen said, 'No, no, they have a right to be here. It isn't a singular universe.'"

"It isn't a singular universe," Derek echoed, "Okay. I'm a quick learner."

He added his cola bottle and sandwich wrappings to the carrier bag.

"What next?"

Susan said, "We drive into Jedburgh. Advertise our presence by promenading the town. If something quite extraordinary is going to happen, then we're warned and aware. If I'm wrong, we'll buy some Jedburgh rock and go home."

"And if you're right?"

"I'll arrest the Earl of Bothwell and his creature and take them back to Newcastle."

Derek and Susan fastened their seat belts almost in unison. The Hummer started smoothly, comfortingly twenty-first century engineering.

"It is a far, far stranger thing that I do now than I have ever done before!" Derek misquoted and Susan laughed.

The car slid from the parking lot onto the carriageway and began to run down the long, green, winding road to Jedburgh.

Derek thought, *Let's hope we buy the rock and go home.*

Susan shivered as someone walked over her grave.

*

The witch was aware of their coming before the Hummer passed the Abbey ruins and turned into High Street. At first as an itching in her forearms that she scratched without thought and then as a dull ache in the breast that drew her from the chair, abandoning embroidery, to compel her onto the street.

In High Street, passing acquaintances without a glance or a word, Margaret Lennox found the intruders turning into the lane that led to the Queen's House. From the railings she watched them enter the porch, somewhat disappointed at their appearance, a middle-aged man and a young woman.

Feeble creatures, thought Margaret Lennox with both contempt and relief, *how dare you think to oppose my son! He will tear you limb from limb and feed your puddens to the hounds.* She settled to wait patiently by the railings in the shadow of the trees.

*

In the guardroom a young man was talking to an older woman and a school group. When Susan and Derek entered he raised a hand in salute, smiled and called brightly, "Give me two minutes!"

"No hurry!" Derek answered.

They listened as the young man concluded his introductory talk to the teacher and her students.

Derek said, quietly, "I thought it was a woman Amy and Paul talked to?"

"Mary MacDonald," Susan agreed, checking her notebook.

The young man came towards them, smiling in welcome.

"Good afternoon! Welcome to the Queen's House! I'm Angus Fleckie. Is this your first visit?"

Susan said, "I'm afraid it's not a visit."

She produced her warrant card. She didn't bother to introduce her companion.

"Oh!" cried Angus, surprised, "Oh, my word! How can I help you?"

Derek said, "We were hoping to talk to a Mary MacDonald?"

"Is she here?" Susan asked.

"Oh, my word! Then you don't know, do you?"

Derek and Susan chorused, "Know what?"

"A terrible tragedy," Angus said and stopped. He seemed near to tears. Susan laid a restraining hand on Derek's arm and said to the young custodian, "Take your time."

"I'm afraid Mary is … dead."

The young man's eyes brimmed with tears.

"It's been a terrible shock," he apologised.

Susan shook her head, "I'm sorry. We didn't know. When did she die?"

"Friday," Angus said and with an unconscious irony, "the thirteenth."

Two days after the twins' visit, thought Sally.

She felt an abrupt shift in understanding. *Nothing is what it seems,* she thought, *no one is what they appear to be.*

Derek said, "What happened?"

"There was a fire. At her cottage."

Training provoked Susan to ask, "Where did the fire start?"

"In the hallway, I understand."

"And Mary was where?"

"She would've been asleep."

Derek interrupted to ask, "What time was this 'accident'?"

"Two, three in the morning. A terrible tragedy! Mary was a lovely woman. A good friend. A great loss to the House."

Derek and Susan exchanged glances.

"The police have any idea what happened?"

Angus lamented, "Sadly Mary was something of an eccentric. She preferred candlelight and oil lamps to electricity."

Derek said, "People like that are usually very careful."

"The source of the fire?" Susan asked.

"An oil lamp. In the hallway."

"Did it fall or was it pushed?" Derek questioned.

Angus was shocked.

"Oh, my word, no! Who on earth would want to hurt Mary?"

"Who indeed?" Susan echoed.

*

Derek Bowman said, "Mary MacDonald was murdered. And nobody is in the least suspicious."

"The Earl of Bothwell always seems to be one step ahead of us," Susan commented.

The ill-assorted pair sat in silence on a bench by the Queen's pear tree.

"He doesn't understand what a terrier he has on his tail."

Susan said, "I'm not sure that's a compliment."

*

Beyond the railings Margaret Lennox waited with a patience honed by centuries of waiting and watching. She smiled as she remembered how the cottage had burned, how ferociously the flames had consumed the centuries-old timber, how the ancient brickwork had crumbled, the moment of triumph when the roof fell in and a fist of flame shot heavenward to strike God's face. Thus was the interfering MacDonald woman extinguished and another tell-tattle tongue silenced. The witch, Bothwell and Cymian had stood silently in the hedge as the fire engine arrived and then walked quietly away.

*

Derek said, "What's frightening is they have no compassion. What harm could this MacDonald woman do to them?"

"Which is all the more reason for you to get into your monster motor and go home," Susan decided.

"Not unless you're coming with me."

"I'm staying tonight."

"Then I'll pin a target on your back. Make sure they don't miss."

"Mary MacDonald didn't know they were after her," Susan asserted.

"I won't be so easy to catch."

Derek stood up and offered Susan a hand to rise.

"Then I'm staying. To watch your back."

*

Mary MacDonald's cottage wasn't difficult to find. At the end of a quiet lane shared with one other cottage, in the midst of a trampled garden was a blackened area of tumbled brickwork, stone and charred beams. A broken chimneypiece stood alone. Derek Bowman and D.C. Susan Duffy stood at the cottage gate and hesitated to enter.

Derek said, "It doesn't seem right to."

Susan lifted aside the damaged gate and walked up the path to where the front door of the cottage had stood. Reluctantly Derek came to join her. The fire had been very greedy. Very little was recognisable. Mary MacDonald and her little world had been effectively extinguished.

"You bastards!" Susan shouted aloud and Derek Bowman was surprisingly shocked at the anger in her words.

To his further surprise, she shouted aloud to the empty air, "I'm going to find you, Bothwell! That's a promise!"

As if embarrassed by this revelation of feeling, Susan snapped, "Let's go! There's nothing here. They've made sure of that."

Derek followed her to the Hummer. He reversed the car and drove slowly down the lane. There was a man standing at the gate of the other cottage who raised a hand in salute and smiled.

"Was he taking the Michael?" Derek snarled, "What the hell is there to smile at? A woman burned to death there!"

"No one," said Sally, "is what they seem. If they want us, they'll know where to find us. But we're not lambs to the slaughter."

THIRTEEN

Derek parked the Hummer in the courtyard behind the Spread Eagle and they approached Reception only to find the outer door locked. They waited and rang again, but in the porter's cubbyhole his radio began to screech with such ear-piercing volume the manager came scurrying from Reception to complain, "For God's sake, Doogie, turn that damn thing doon! I cannae hear maself think!"

But to their mutual astonishment the radio couldn't be silenced until the two strangers outside had given up ringing the bell and retired, defeated.

"We'll leave the car here," Derek decided, "and find a B&B."

Susan agreed, but cast backward glances to the hotel that had every appearance of life except the door to Reception was locked and no one answered the porter's bell.

On the street they stopped a middle-aged woman and asked where they might find the best Bed and Breakfast.

"Oh, you'll find guid BBs in Jesmond Road," she told Derek, with an arch smile, "I ken yi'll no be wanting to take home any chats? It's Jesmond Road you're wanting right enough."

Much of which was incomprehensible to Derek.

"Jesmond Road?" said Sally, "Where's that then?"

"No more'n a hop and a skip from here," the woman said and gave directions.

As they walked Derek asked, "What's chats?"

"Fleas."

Derek pondered as they walked.

"Do these people not like us?"

"Why'd you ask?"

"She seemed to find us amusing."

Susan said, "You have an English accent. You talk posh."

"So what are you?"

"A Geordie copper. Soon's I opened me gob she'd know what I was."

In the back of her mind Susan heard a warning bell ring, not loudly nor persistently, but the bell did ring and Susan heard it ring.

"Describe the woman we've just spoken to," she demanded of Derek.

Derek hesitated.

"Describe her."

"Just a woman. Middle-aged? Grey hair?"

He looked to Susan who shook her head.

"I've no idea," she confessed, "And I'm supposed to."

Derek said comfortingly, "As long as she hasn't sent us astray."

The woman's directions were accurate, but it was rather more than a hop and a skip. Susan suspected they were being given the run-around, but said nothing.

They found Jesmond Road to be a fine avenue of Victorian triple-storey houses. Number seventeen had a card in the window signifying vacancies, but when Susan and Derek rang and were answered, the landlady turned them away.

As their footsteps faded from her path, Mrs. Morrison, in the silence of her hallway, found herself puzzled and somewhat frightened. The words that came from her mouth were not the welcome she had phrased in her head.

Now, whatever came over me? Sending them away like that, respectable folk. No need for me to speak to them like that. She wasn't that sort of young woman.

Missis Morrison went into her sitting room and broke her own rules, pouring herself a glass of ruby port. Remembering a magazine article she had read recently she was suddenly frightened. *May be I'm losing my mind?* She poured a second glass of port and her hand trembled.

At number twenty-three, Derek would've sworn the card in the window said VACANCIES, but when they approached the door it read NO VACANCIES.

"I would've sworn," said Derek, but Susan had been checking her text messages.

"Next door," Susan said, "Family Hotel. Sounds a bit posher than B and B."

Derek rang the bell.

Now she had drawn them to her front door, Margaret Lennox waited until the second ring before going to answer the bell. *The cat will let the mouse run. Tis all part and parcel of the game.* She fastened a smile to her face and went to answer the door.

The middle-aged man and the young woman stood on the doorstep. The man was tired, but he dug up a smile. The witch sensed the young woman's mind was buzzing like a beehive.

"We were hoping you might have vacancies?" the man said.

Margaret Lennox smiled, playing with two tense and tired people.

"Have you tried the Spread Eagle? Perhaps that's more what you're seeking?"

The man smiled ruefully and replied, "Couldn't get an answer."

"We're very simple here," admitted the witch slyly, "Have you tried Mrs. MacDonald's at the corner? I hear she has a hot tub. Although we do have baths, of course."

"No vacancies, I'm afraid," said the young woman.

"But there was no room at the inn," the man said, attempting humour, "I don't suppose you have a stable?"

"You've no come on horseback?" Margaret Lennox asked, playing the innocent.

The man is a fool. Does he think to charm his way into the charnel house? The witch played with them as a cat with a mouse, not knowing how much they knew or guessed. *But I will know, I will peep and pry until I know. Then we will see what's to be done.*

"Just a joke," said the man, weakly.

"Now why would you be coming to Jethart?"

The young woman said, "We came on impulse. To get away for a few days."

But she was thinking, *What the hell business is it of yours?*

The witch reaching into her mind faced an unexpected sword and retreated, cursing.

"Ah, you're English, of course," said the witch, smarting at the unseen rebuff, "the English now they're always fond of jokes. Though mind, I am too myself. Who doesn't like a guid laugh now and then?"

Looking at this middle-aged woman, a face you'd never remember in a hundred years. Four hundred years? Derek thought, *Come on, you stupid woman! Yes or no?*

"How long would you be staying?"

Susan said, "We're not sure. A few days?"

Steaming puddens, easier getting into Russia before glastnost than this!

Susan thought, *This woman's a bitch. There's malice here.*

Turning away, she said, "We'll find somewhere. Thanks, anyway."

"Wait," said the witch, "I'll not be turning you away. I'm not one for casuals. But I doubt there's an empty bed in the town with the Riding."

They looked at one another, Susan and Derek, the young woman thinking, *I don't like this woman, there's darkness here,* and the man thinking, *We're going to end up with paranoia, jumping at every shadow. She's just a bitchy landlady.*

But the worm of unease persisted still.

"I have my weeklies, you understand, but mostly returners. And Mister Campbell's been with me since the year dot, but he's no trouble at all."

Is it really worth trudging on up the street? thought Derek Bowman.

"We'd be no more trouble than Mr. Campbell," Susan said.

My feet are killing me. Just give me somewhere to flop down.

"You'll not be wanting a double room?" the witch asked, casting a disapproving eye, "I'll have none of that here. There'll be no hanky-panky here. This is a respectable house."

Susan laughed and shook her head.

"And we don't need a connecting door either, Missis...?"

"Miss Lennox, if you please."

"Single rooms will be fine, Miss Lennox," Derek agreed.

"Then come yourselves in."

*

The doctor returned to her patient and placed the swaddled babe into the waiting arms of his mother.

"James the first of England, sixth of Scotland, your Majesty," she said aloud, quite unselfconsciously, and laughed.

Mary responded with a smile, whispering, "Merci, madame, merci."

"Born," said Doctor Bowman, "not in a royal palace, but in a Victorian terrace in Gosforth, Newcastle upon Tyne. Not many people know that."

She reached to stroke away the wet hair on Mary's brow, rewarded by a smile, and said, "Now then, your Majesty, we'll tidy you up."

The doctor continued, "I think, Majesty, perhaps no one will notice if I fix you with a drip. Better than leeches."

How odd, thought Joyce Bowman, *that I find nothing odd about this situation. I am surprised by nothing any more.*

When her tasks were completed she sat in the chair by the sleeping Queen, burdened with fatigue, but sleepless and wept quietly, not for Mary and her shipwrecked child, but for her own children, far beyond her help, far beyond her love.

*

Will you walk into my parlour, said the spider to the fly, It's the prettiest little parlour that ever you may spy. The way into my parlour is up a winding stair, and I have many curious things to show when you are there.

Reluctantly, Susan Duffy and Derek Bowman crossed the threshold following the landlady, Margaret Lennox. In the hallway, Susan caught the faintest whiff of decay before Summer Lavender overpowered her nostrils. Susan looked to Derek who grimaced and whispered, "Let's just be glad of a bed."

Susan nodded, whispering, "P'rhaps a connecting door would be a comfort?"

At the foot of the stairs Susan stopped. A cat peered at the intruders from the upper landing.

Susan said aloud, "Oh, hell, a cat! I can't bear cats," and shivered involuntarily, thinking, *What a wuss! But I can't help it. They give me the creeps.*

The cat, curiosity satisfied, sauntered from sight, but Miss Lennox ahead of them, ears of a bat, missed nothing.

"Will you be wanting dinner?"

Why not? said Susan's shoulders.

"Thank you, yes," Derek said, resigned to the worst, surrendering, "if it's no bother."

The witch said, "Oh, I doubt you'll trouble me too much, Mister Bowman. It'll only be shepherd's pie, but I use a guid butcher. I could do you tinned peaches and ice cream to follow? "

"That's very kind," Derek said.

Susan thought, *That's odd. She knows his name. Did we say who we were?*

As they climbed beyond the first landing Susan listened to the house creaking, whispering, listening, noisy in its silence, breath stinking of decay.

"Here we are then, Miss Duffy," offered Margaret Lennox as she opened a bedroom door, "Number nine. I'm often complimented on it being my nicest room. You'll have the sunshine in the morning."

Susan, peered into a very ordinary room, bed, dressing table, chair, and thought, *Did I tell her my name?*

"Your friend'll be over the landing in number thirteen. I'd appreciate it if you didn't allow him into your room after ten."

"D'y'bang a gong at ten?" Derek asked and Margaret Lennox smiled.

"Don't think I don't know you're teasing me," said the landlady, "I'm no stookie, but this is a Christian household."

"Amen to that," Derek answered, "Just what we were looking for. I'll brush up on my Catechism."

Susan struggled not to laugh, but Margaret Lennox said, "Your friend has a grand sense of humour. I like that in a man."

"Behave, Derek," Susan said.

"I'll bring you fresh towels in a wee while, Miss Duffy."

Susan started to say, "How do you know?" but stopped.

"Is there something else you're wanting?"

"No," Susan said, "nothing. Thank you."

Thinking, *I didn't tell her my name. I'm sure I didn't.*

"Then I'll leave you to settle in. I'll call you when supper is ready."

*

"I'm sure you must be weary, dear, with soaring up so high, will you rest upon my little bed?" said the spider to the fly, "There are pretty curtains drawn around; the sheets are fine and thin, and if you like to rest awhile, I'll snugly tuck you in!"

*

As he opened his overnight case, Derek Bowman, in a flash of intuition, realised there was no one else in the house. He stopped moving and stood still, unbreathing, listening. The silence was absolute. There were no feet on the stairs of boarders returning from work. No snatches of speech, laughter, coughing from any neighbouring room. No one in the house dropped a shoe or switched on music. No one was listening to the News. There were no weeklies and no Returners. There was no Mister Campbell, here since the Year Dot.

Derek opened his bedroom door and stepped out onto the landing. From below drifted the stale smell of boiled cabbage. First tapping on and then opening the adjacent doors of bedrooms, he found all empty. As far as he could tell there was not a sign of occupancy. The house was empty of life.

"Would there be something you're wanting, Mr. Bowman?"

Soft and silent as cat's paws, Miss Lennox stood behind him, with an armful of towels.

"God, but you made me jump!" Derek cried, alarmed.

"Was there something you were seeking, Mr. Bowman?"

"Sorry. The bathroom?"

"You'll find it behind the door marked BATHROOM. Jist ahind you."

"Oh, thank you. Foolish of me."

Derek stood aside as Margaret Lennox entered the bathroom and deposited her towels.

"I'd be grateful if you didn't leave the hot taps dripping," said the landlady, brushing against him as she politely held open the bathroom door for Derek to enter. What Derek Bowman didn't see was the spiderlike creature that crawled up his back to the collar.

Derek waited in the bathroom for the silent feet to melt away and then stepped out on to the landing again to warn Susan that the house was empty. Then suddenly, it didn't seem important any more. Seeing her door shut, he hesitated to knock and returned to his own room.

Daft, that's what I am, daft. What the hell does it matter? I could do with fifty winks. Doubtless a bloody great gong'll sound for supper. Or a blast on the bagpipes.

Derek lay down on the bed and slipped from drowsiness to dozing. Sliding into sleep he became aware, but only just aware, that someone or something had come into room thirteen. But Derek didn't move, couldn't move. He couldn't stir a finger or toe. His eyelids were as heavy as lead coffin lids. Then the nightmare began with a whisper.

*

"Sweet creature!" said the spider, "You're witty and you're wise;
How handsome are your gauzy wings; how brilliant are your eyes!
I have a little looking glass upon my parlour shelf
If you'd step in a moment, dear, you shall behold yourself."

*

In room nine, Detective Constable Susan Duffy was imprisoned. She sat hunched up on the bed, keeping very still, humming, with arms locked about her legs, hiding her head, hands clutching her toes. When she came back from the bathroom it was there.

I have this phobia about cats, y'see. Ever since I was a kid. Stupid, isn't it? I know it's stupid, but I can't help it, Mammy. Please don't let it get me. I'll be good. I promise. I won't ever wet the bed again.

She wanted to scream, but she couldn't. A fearful moan was all her throat allowed. A hairless cat sat jailor against her bedroom door, licking its shoulder, saliva glistening like a snail trail.

I have this phobia. About cats. I know any minute now. That thing. Is going to jump up on the bed and eat my toes. Don't laugh. It's not funny. When it does I'll scream until I die.

FOURTEEN

"It is such a shame," Tina reflected, "She is a very nice lady. I like her."

Joyce Bowman and Tina, her new 'house-help' as she styled herself, sat at the kitchen table with coffee and the biscuits Tina had brought to share. Her real name Joyce had stumbled over too often. They both agreed Tina was a suitable abbreviation. Preparations for the evening meal were complete. Their coffee break was well deserved and they relaxed in each other's company.

"That's why it must be kept confidential," Joyce explained, "A private matter. She is a very important lady, but sadly, her health." Joyce left the sentence unfinished and Tina nodded gravely.

"I understand," she said, "You can rely on me. Mum's the word."

"Majesty is the word," Joyce said and smiled, "She believes she's a Queen and so we'll treat her as a queen."

"No problem," Tina said, "I understand. I say Majesty when I speak to her. I can do the knee bending. A very nice lady. And baby James is so sweet."

"Which reminds me," Joyce said, glancing at the kitchen clock, "I'll go get the young prince while you prepare his royal bottle."

Tina laughed and both rose from the table. At the kitchen door, Joyce Bowman hesitated to say, "Remember! No one must know Missis Stuart and her baby are here. We don't want newspaper reporters sniffing around. There's only you and me here."

"I understand," Tina said, "In my country we learn when to keep our mouths shut."

Tina was spooning the baby formula into a jug when the doorbell rang. She waited, but when the bell rang urgently she went to answer the summons. When she opened the door a dark-haired bearded man stood on the doorstep.

Tina asked, "Can I help you?"

The man hesitated as if surprised to see her and said, "I need to speak to Doctor Bowman."

"Why?" asked Tina.

The man's face darkened.

"That is none of your business."

Tina said, "Yes, it is. I am her househelp."

"Bring Doctor Bowman to the door."

Behind the shield of the door, Tina's right hand tightened into a fist.

"No. Doctor is not seeing anyone. She has not been very well."

"She would see me. Let me come in."

Tina shook her head and said, "No."

For a moment the young woman thought the visitor was about to force his way into the house and tensed herself to resist. The man sensed her resolve and relaxed.

"You ought to be ashamed of yourself," Tina admonished him, "You know the doctor has had a very sad time."

"I would only wish to offer my good wishes."

"I'll tell her your good wishes."

"Has the doctor anyone staying with her, a friend perhaps? That is a comfort in such times."

Tina shook her head.

"There is only the doctor and myself."

"No one else?"

"No. She wants to be quiet."

The dark-haired man turned away from the door.

"What is your name?" Tina called, "Who should I say called?"

The visitor ignored her and crossed to the car parked at the farther kerb. Tina watched as he started the engine. With a clashing of gears he drove away. Blue smoke drifted from the exhaust of the old Morris Traveller. The young woman thought she saw a child in the back seat staring at her.

As she closed the door Joyce Bowman came down the stairs carrying the baby James.

"Who was at the door?"

"A reporter. He wanted to come in. Let him try. I would have kicked him in the privates!"

138

Despite herself, Joyce Bowman laughed aloud.

"Well done, Tina! I didn't know I'd hired a bodyguard."

They went into the kitchen together to feed the baby. As she watched the young woman nurse the infant, Joyce's mind clouded with apprehension, but she smiled in response to Tina's simple happiness as she looked up from the baby.

"I've just noticed," Joyce Bowman said, "You have eyes of two different colours. The left gray. The right blue. Quite rare. Heterochromia iridium."

"It's a family thing," Tina explained, "My sisters too. I didn't know it had such a big name."

"Heterochromia iridium," Joyce repeated, and Tina sang it to the baby.

"He tero chro mia iridi um dum dum!"

Joyce felt her fear fading, the clouds retreating.

When they retired for the night, Tina struggled to shoot top and bottom bolts on both front and back doors. The bolts had not been used for some years. Tina persisted despite Joyce's reassurances as to the dead locks.

"Just in case," said Tina.

"In case of what?"

"Reporters," Tina affirmed, "They are not gentlemen. We do not want to come downstairs to find them eating breakfast in the kitchen."

Joyce was surprised to find herself laughing aloud.

"Tina," she said, "Why didn't I find you sooner?"

*

John Traquair, Captain of the Queen's Guard, came into the outer chamber of the Queen's bedchamber as Paul said, "Agreed that the pretence of her Majesty's presence in the House be maintained?"

All knew if the House were overrun many innocent lives would be lost for this deception. There was a murmur of agreement from Adam Blackwood and Mary Seton. As he sat down to company, the Captain asked, hesitantly, "Her Majesty is alive?"

Amy smiled to reassurd him, "The Queen still lives."

"There will be other babies," mourned Mary Seton, seeking comfort, "God willing."

Amy took her hand to say, "The baby lives. It's a boy."

"James the Sixth of Scotland," said Paul, but stopped when Amy looked at him.

Sharing glances with Traquair and Mary Seton, the Secretary asked, "Where are they, my lady? The Queen and her child?"

"They are safe," Paul assured him.

"Where?" asked the Captain.

"In another place," Amy said, "A safe place."

Mary Seton, wide-eyed, asked, "In Heaven?"

Amy smiled, "When I was younger I thought it was."

Paul said, "I suggest, Captain, we keep Bothwell guessing. You must go out under flag of truce and plead for a doctor to visit the Queen."

John Traquair laughed and cried, "Excellent!"

"They'll refuse, of course," the Secretary warned.

"So beg them," Amy insisted, "We want them to believe we're desperate."

*

"Did you think we'd let you meddle in our business?" asked Margaret Lennox, "You have no place here. You are as a child under men's feet. A manikin!"

Bound to the bed with invisible bonds, Derek Bowman found he could stir neither hand nor foot.

"You wish to say something?"

Derek found his tongue loosened. He struggled to speak, but failed to control his tongue.

"Speak up!" his tormentor demanded, "I give you license yet you have nothing to say?"

Derek felt his throat tighten and close. Breath cut off, he began to panic, heart pounding, eyes bulging. Then the iron grip was loosed again as he gasped for breath.

"Speak, my dear bowman," the witch coaxed, "I delight in good conversation."

Derek, heart pounding, struggled to croak, "Why have you murdered my children? My son. My daughter. What have they ever done to you?"

"Mary it is that's earned the title of murderer," Margaret Lennox retorted, "My son. My handsome son was murdered. But they will not succeed! How close they are they know not. Elizabeth is at Newcastle upon the Tyne. So near and yet so far. But they shall not succeed! They will believe Elizabeth has departed. But a broken axle holds her in Newcastle yet. So they will not succeed!"

Baffled, uncomprehending, Derek asked, "Succeed in what?"

"Mary, Queen of Scots, will still go to the block at Fotheringhay. Shall I tell you how it was?"

Derek Bowman nodded, struggling to comprehend the incomprehensible. The woman spoke with glee, savouring every moment.

"She laid her head upon the block. Stretched out her arms and legs. When she was lying quite still, Bull's man put his hand on her body to steady it for the blow."

Margaret Lennox licked her lips in anticipation of triumph, eyes fast upon another place, another time. Derek Bowman thought, *The web slackens. When her mind is elsewhere I can move. A finger. A hand.*

"Even so," said Margaret, Countess of Lennox, rapt in the telling, re-telling of her enemy's death, "the first blow missed her neck."

Her face was gleeful. *I can move*, thought Derek Bowman, *Easy now. Don't let her.*

"The axe missed her precious neck and cut into the back of her head. She was not to have an easy death. Her lips moved. She said, 'Sweet Jesus!' in the smallest voice. But the second blow severed the neck. All but the smallest sinew."

Derek Bowman tensed himself for the supreme effort.

*

Joyce Bowman awoke, struggling for breath, striving to free herself from the strong hand that sealed her mouth. A voice whispered in her ear.

"Excuse me, doctor," Tina urged, "Forgive me disturbing you, but you must be very quiet. A man is trying to enter the house."

The hand left her mouth and Joyce fought for breath.

"Have you phoned the police?"

"No."

Joyce struggled to rise, but the young woman restrained her.

"That would not be the best thing to do," Tina advised.

"Of course, we must phone the police! This isn't Russia! This is England!"

Joyce reached for the bedside telephone, but Tina caught her hand.

"No police, please. Not with Missis Stuart in the house. And the baby. We do not want police here."

Joyce relaxed and Tina brought the doctor her dressing gown.

"He has managed to open the locks on the front door, but found the door bolted. He is very angry."

Joyce Bowman asked, "Tina, what do you know about Missis Stuart?"

"What you have told me. She is a very important lady and she has been very ill."

I don't believe you, the doctor thought, *Too coincidental that you turn up when I need you.*

"Where is he now?"

"The kitchen door. He is trying to open the lock."

Thank God for the bolts, Joyce thought, *Would I have struggled to shoot them unless Tina were here?*

"What I would like you to do, doctor, please," said Tina, "is to go to Missis Stuart's room. So she and the baby will not be disturbed. If you will forgive me for telling you what to do, please?"

"And what will you do?"

"I will go and ask this man to stop trying to get into the house."

Joyce Bowman almost laughed.

"If it is he who killed my children, asking him won't work."

"He will not disturb you, doctor," Tina said, "If the baby wakes there is a bottle prepared in the warming machine in the dressing room."

On the landing they parted, the doctor to the Queen's room and Tina down the dark stairs.

*

The naked cat stared at the traumatised young policewoman, trembling against the bedhead.

You are not a child, thought Susan Duffy and then said aloud, "I am not a child."

The cat twitched its whiskers and stared at her. It felt good to say it aloud. But the fear still churned within her. *No one who hasn't felt this fear can know how I feel.* The cat licked its bare shoulder again and Susan shuddered. She fought the urge to hide her head again.

I am not a child. I am a trained police officer. Ay. Cee. Tee. I will Ay. assess the situation. Cee. Caution the alleged offender. Tee. Take action. Ay. Cee. Tee. Act! What are you afraid of, Sue? Say it out loud. I'm afraid . . .

"I'm afraid the cat will eat my toes," she whispered.

Her stomach churned. Her chin fell to her chest.

"I know it will!"

Sue, listen to me! On the bedside table there's a vase. Reach for it. Got it? Now, if the cat tries to . . . if the cat gets on the bed, hit it with the vase. All right? Now. Caution the alleged offender.

Susan Duffy, clutching the vase, giggled.

"Cat! Cat, d'y'hear me? I want to go out the door!" Susan shouted, "If you try to stop me, I'll belt you with this!"

Susan shook the vase at the cat, but the cat didn't move. It sat staring at her. The young woman began to feel chill fear grow again.

"Now. Take action. I can't. Yes, you can! I can't. I can't. I'm afraid. Listen to me, Sue! Move your feet. Over the side of the bed. On to the floor. I can't! The cat will eat my toes. Don't be so silly! It will, I know it will. Don't look at the cat. Just do it!"

Slowly, fearfully, the young woman lowered her feet to the floor. *Stand up, Sue! Stand up!* Shakily, Susan Duffy stood up. *Now act! Go to the door. If the cat tries to stop you. Brain the bloody thing!*

With fearful footsteps, Susan approached the cat, clutching the vase. The cat didn't move. Suddenly, she saw the creature wasn't real. When Susan bent down, incredulous, and poked the loathsome object with the vase, it fell apart into fragments of mouldering skin and bone.

With the stink of decay in her nostrils, Susan, shuddering, kicked the mummified remnants into a corner.

*

The young woman called Tina heard the deadlock click as the intruder succeeded and the kitchen door was unlocked. Someone bellowed in triumph.

"Whoever you are," Tina called, "you had best leave now. You will not harm the doctor. You will not enter this house."

There was silence and then a man spoke.

"Who are you?"

"You have killed her children. Is that not enough?"

"I will not hurt the doctor. But I will search the house."

Tina said, "I don't believe you. You destroy whoever is in your path. But there is no one to search for. There is the doctor and me."

The intruder hurled his weight against the door, but the bolts stood firm. Tina listened to his cursing.

"You will not enter this house," the young woman repeated.

His body weight slammed against the door in frustration rather than expectation. She listened to his heavy breathing and then he spoke indistinctly to someone. There was silence broken only by the passing of a car. Tina became aware the intruder and his companion, companions, were no longer outside the kitchen door. She moved swiftly to the hallway and listened to the silence of the house.

The young woman ran upstairs quickly and opened the Queen's bedroom door. Mary Stuart lay sleeping soundly. Tina opened the dressing room door. Joyce Bowman sat in the nursing chair feeding the baby.

Tina said, "All is well. Keep calm and carry on." She was proud of her colloquial English. As she descended the stairs she heard glass breaking.

When she flew down the last flight of stairs into the hallway, she saw the coloured glass of the narrow window beside the front door had been broken. A dwarf in chain mail was struggling to open the bottom bolt. As Tina approached the dwarf, he unsheathed his sword and said, "Take out the bolts, girl. My master wishes to enter."

Tina said, "Your master will not enter."

The young woman walked to within sword reach of the dwarf.

"How deep must I cut you before you obey?"

Cymian snarled and swung the sword tip within an inch of Tina's face. The young woman didn't flinch. Before surprise registered on the dwarf's face, Tina asked, "What's wrong with your hand, little man?"

Cymian glanced at his left hand. His little finger was burning with a clear yellow flame. One after another his fingers began to blister and burn. His hand and then his arm began to peel and burn as a torch flares. Cymian screamed in agony and screamed again in terror. Tina unbolted the front door and opened it. No one attempted to enter. The dwarf stared with bulging eyes at the young woman, screaming as the inferno reached his shoulder and his hair began to sizzle.

Cymian ran to the open door, crying, "Master, the witch has killed me!"

When he crossed the threshold the flames died as if they had never been. Cymian stood dumbfounded, staring at his arm.

"Good night, little man," Tina said. She closed, locked and bolted the door.

She arrived at the dressing room to find Joyce Bowman winding a contented, sleepy baby over her shoulder.

To Joyce's silent enquiry, she answered, "They have gone."

*

Crossbowmen stood either side of the open door as Blackwood and Traquair climbed the ladder back into the House. Paul offered a hand and pulled them one after the other into the safety of the hall.

Amy asked, "They refused?"

John Traquair agreed, "They refused. As we knew they would."

"We begged them," Adam Blackwood said, "Begged them for the mercy of a doctor."

"They were delighted we were so desperate."

"But we denounced them as murderers," Traquair declared.

Adam Blackwood said, "John was magnificent! The Queen is our lawful sovereign! Should any harm come to her Majesty, I warn you!

Hide yourselves well! You will be hunted to the end of your days! You could sense unease among the men."

"However, they agreed no one should starve," Traquair added, "There are women bringing bread."

John Blackwood hastened to say, "We are well provisioned, but we must appear to be in need."

As he spoke three women carrying baskets on their backs hurried from the trampled garden below the House and approached the ladder.

"Come up!" Traquair commanded and the women began to climb.

"Milady," suggested Mary Seton, "if you would retire from direct view?"

Amy went to sit on Mary's chair at the end of the hall. To her surprise Mary Seton bundled up a shawl and placed it in her lap.

"What're you-?" Amy began to say, but Mary said, "It is Lord Paul's instruction."

The marie cushioned Amy about with shawls and then stood at her elbow.

"You are very pregnant, milady," Mary said and smiled.

The first woman climbing into the hall looked about her and seeing Amy in shadow immediately bobbed the knee and lowered her head. As a surprised Amy moved to rise, Mary's arm restrained her.

"She mistakes you for her Majesty," Mary whispered, "That will do no harm."

A kitchen maid took the basket of bread from the bearer who stood by as two more women climbed into the House. They both acknowledged Amy. Kitchen maids returned the empty baskets to the bearers who began to descend the ladder under the watchful eye of the crossbowmen. But the third woman lingered to speak to Adam Blackwood.

"Master," she said, "May I speak with you?"

"Speak freely."

"I was of her Majesty's household."

She bobbed her head in Amy's direction.

"Yes?"

"The Queen's husband."

"Lord Darnley. Yes?"

The woman hesitated.

The iron-shod clogs of the women on the ladder could clearly be heard, rung-by-rung.

Blackwood said, "Speak up, woman! No one here will do you harm."

"Lord Darnley is in lodgings at the Spread Eagle."

"The Devil he is!" cried Traquair, "Then why has he not come to her Majesty's aid?"

"He is presently quitting Jethart to retire to Edinburgh."

"Leaving the Queen at the mercy of Bothwell? Surely not!"

A woman's voice cried from the foot of the ladder.

"Martha!"

"I must go, master," the woman said.

She bobbed again to Amy and cried, "God bless your Majesty!"

She began to descend the ladder.

"When will he go?" Adam Blackwood demanded.

"Even now he is preparing to leave," the woman said.

They watched her climb down the ladder to join the women at its foot. The three women ran off together. The ladder was swiftly pulled up into the hall and the door safely shut and barred.

Adam Blackwood said, "Well done, milady! They will redouble their effort to assail us now they are assured the Queen is in the House."

Amy punched Paul.

"You might have told me!"

"And if they succeed?" Paul questioned.

John Traquair said, "We will rebuke any attempt to breach the House."

Amy asked, "But if they do break in?"

Adam Blackwood said, "They will kill everyone, milady."

*

Standing at the kitchen sink filling the kettle Joyce Bowman noticed movement under the old beech tree at the end of the garden. Alarm flared and water overflowed the kettle. When the figure moved Joyce realised it was Tina.

"Now what?" she said aloud, realising the young woman knelt where the stillborn princess lay. Her heart rate began to climb again. *How would she know? Is it so obvious it's a grave? Couldn't it be a pet grave?*

Joyce rescued the kettle, set it to boil, dried her hands and went to join Tina.

Under the shade of the old tree the young woman was planting bulbs from a trug on to the barely discernable mound of disturbed earth. Tina smiled up at the doctor. Joyce watched as the task was completed. Tina stood up and dusted off her hands.

"Her name," said the young woman, "would have been Mathilde. She would have married a Dauphin of France and borne seven children. But that is in another time, another place. Today she sleeps under a beech tree in an English garden."

The two women walked back to the house together.

FIFTEEN

"Why have I had you brought before me?" James Hepburn, Earl of Bothwell demanded.

The three serving women shook their heads and counted their toes.

"Answer the lord," Cymian ordered.

"Don't know, lord," the woman called Charity muttered without raising her head.

"Would it be the mutton, lord?" suggested the oldest woman, "I told Sarah it wasn't."

"Because it is said," Bothwell interrupted, "You have seen the Queen."

The three women exchanged relieved glances.

"You saw the Queen?" Bothwell demanded.

The three women nodded agreement.

"Tell me," said Bothwell.

"She was sitting in her chair, lord," said Charity, "At the end of the hall."

"Who was with her?"

"Her marie."

"Mary Seton," said Hannah.

"You know the woman?"

"I was of the Queen's household, lord."

"You saw her clearly?"

The women exchanged glances.

Jane said, "We were at a distance, lord, but who else would sit in the Queen's chair?"

The women waited in a nervous silence.

"You," said Bothwell, "the woman of the Queen's household. Your name?"

"Hannah," she answered, trembling.

"It was the Queen in the hall?"

"Yes, lord. She was silent, but they all looked to her."

"The Queen is heavy with child?"

"She is so."

"She was shawled and did not look in good health, lord."

"Her face is thin."

Bothwell pondered on the answers.

"Very well. You may go."

The women chorused, "Thank you, lord," and moved to leave.

Cymian whispered into his master's ear.

"Wait!" said Bothwell and the women stopped, turning frightened faces to their lord.

"Which of you was last down the ladder?"

"I was," confessed Hannah, raising a trembling hand.

"You will stay," Bothwell commanded.

Jane and Charity fled from his presence.

The serving woman called Hannah stood trembling before her lord in his chair. Beyond the walls she could hear voices, horses and the rattle of carriage wheels. Bothwell had chosen the Toll House on the Edinburgh road as his quarters. No one passed to the capital or to England without his consent. In the silence she heard the hound at Bothwell's feet yawn and stretch without lifting her eyes. When Cymian whispered in his master's ear she began to shake. Every servant knew of the cruelties Cymian employed to entertain his master.

"Are you afraid, Hannah?"

"Yes, lord."

"Why?"

Hannah hesitated and whispered, "I don't know, lord, but I am afraid."

"You're fearful of being whipped for not telling me the truth?"

"Yes, lord."

"Tell me the truth and you have nothing to fear."

Hannah nodded, overcome with relief.

"Yes, lord."

"Why did you leave the Queen's household?"

"I fell pregnant. There was no place for me."

Cymian giggled and Hannah shivered.

"Where is the child?"

"The baby died, lord."

Cymian laughed and said, slyly, "I wager she smothered the brat!"

"No!" Hannah cried, "On my soul I would not! The child had a fever and died."

She forgot herself so far as to raise her head and glare hatred at the dwarf.

"Why did you linger in the House when the others had gone?"

Hannah's heart beat as a kettledrum in alarm.

"It was the Captain, Earl Traquair, lord."

"Ah!" said Bothwell, "The good captain of the bodyguard! Perchance, he wished to arrange a tryst with you?"

Cymian tittered and Hannah recognised her peril.

"He asked me," Hannah lied, "how many soldiers there were."

"And?"

"How many horses. If you had a cannon. If any siege ladders were being prepared."

"And how did you answer?"

"I said I didn't know. Because I don't know, lord."

"Why would he think you would answer his questions?"

Hannah hesitated as if reluctant to speak.

"He said if I would find the answers to his questions, I would be taken into the Queen's household again."

"He knew you?"

"The Queen's marie knew me."

"How would you answer his questions?"

"When we next deliver bread, lord."

In the silence Hannah prayed fervently to herself. Her bladder was overflowing and the beating of her heart must awaken the dead.

Cymian said, "Let me take the woman and test her answers, lord."

Hannah screamed silently, all colour drained from her face. *I am a dead woman,* she thought, *I am a dead woman, God help me!*

"No," said Bothwell, "She tells the truth. But there will be no more bread."

"Thank you, lord," Hannah cried, "Thank you!"

She flung herself at Bothwell's feet. Her magnanimous lord kicked her away.

"You may go," he said and Hannah fled.

Cymian stood scowling after her.

"The Jethart woman who stole bread from Robsart's wagon?" James Hepburn, Earl of Bothwell enquired.

"She is yet to be flogged as you directed, lord."

"Flog her and hang her where they can hear and see her die from the House. They shall have their answer."

Cymian pranced gleefully, his face alight with pleasure.

"Thank you, lord! I shall have her dance for an hour before she dies!"

*

While the witch spoke Derek Bowman felt the web slacken. *When her mind is elsewhere I can move. A finger. A hand.*

"When her head fell," said Margaret, Countess of Lennox, "Mary's body tried to stand up. Struggled to stand up and fell backwards. Her lap dog ran out of her skirts, yelping to be kicked to shut its yap. I have never laughed so much. If I were to tell you that day was the happiest day of my life. That woman killed my son. I rejoiced in her death."

The witch was rapt in the telling of her sorry tale. Her face was gleeful.

I can move, thought Derek Bowman, *Easy now. Don't let her.*

"Did you know," said Margaret Lennox, "that the head does not die when it is cut off? It lives a time or so. When I picked up that woman's head, she was looking at me. She knew me. I saw the terror in her eyes. I let her see her body lying in its piss."

Margaret Lennox laughed for the joy of it.

"I have seen many executions, but this was the pearl of all!"

My God, thought Derek Bowman, *you'd think she was telling a child a bedtime story.*

But when he tried to leap up his body was aflame with pain and Margaret Lennox mocked him.

"You think to catch an old fox with stale meat, my poor archer? You will stay and listen until I am done. And then you will be undone, I promise."

152

Suddenly, behind the witch, Derek Bowman saw the bedroom door begin to open. Susan Duffy slid silently into the room. Derek began to struggle against the binding web to hold the witch's attention. Susan crept slowly towards his tormentor.

"Be still, you foolish man! Or I will give you cause for regret!"

Derek saw Susan wore a colourful vase on her right arm. He felt an almost irresistible urge to laugh that he immediately regretted. The witch read his face and sprang about to confront the young detective.

*

Mary Seton said, "Lord Darnley is only un petit roi."

"A small king?" Paul questioned, "How small?"

John Traquair laughed.

"It's not about the measure of the man."

"The Queen has refused the crown matrimonial to Lord Darnley," Adam Blackwood explained, "Henry Darnley is merely a pawn. Tied to his mother's apron strings."

"And who is she?" Amy asked.

"His mother is Margaret, Countess of Lennox."

John Traquair said, "A very dangerous woman. She is believed to be in league with Satan. The Countess would have the Queen dead and her own grandson likewise, to enthrone Henry Darnley as King of Scotland."

Amy and Paul were horrified.

"She would kill her own grandson?" Amy exclaimed.

Adam Blackwood said, "She would kill a thousand, thousand to attain her ends."

"Thank God the Queen and the baby are out of her reach," Paul submitted.

"May I remind you, lord, our enemies believe they are here. Under siege in the House," commented John Traquair, "By his quitting Jethart, Darnley has signalled to Bothwell, by-my-leave you may murder the Queen and my son. I stand aside. Do what you will."

"May God preserve us all from such evil," Mary Seton prayed.

"Amen to that," echoed Adam Blackwood.

A chill silence fell upon the outer chamber. Amy, looking around at the sombre faces, was struck by sudden memory. *Maybe A Levels are good for something after all!*

Racking her brains to remember Antonia Fraser's book, Amy cried, "Darnley will be lodged at Kirk o' Field."

Blackwood and Traquair exchanged glances.

Adam said, "You are well-informed, milady. The air is thought by physicians to be the most salubrious in the town."

"He will be murdered there," Amy announced.

Mary Seton cried, in horror, "The King? Milady, surely not!"

"Am I right, Paul?"

Paul nodded agreement.

"Murdered by Bothwell. There is no honour among thieves."

"Can you foresee such tragedy?" Adam Blackwood asked, wonderingly.

"And the Queen will be blamed for his death," Paul added.

"Kirk o' Field is most secure," John Traquair argued, "His own household. A strong town watch."

"He will die at Kirk o' Field," said Amy, "Unless we can persuade him not to leave Jethart, but to aid his Queen and save his crown."

"Then you must go to him, milady," Mary Seton decided, "And my Lord Paul. Persuade his Majesty otherwise."

Mary and the Queen's officers looked expectantly to the twins.

Amy smiled to explain, "We are restricted to this house as you are."

"We cannot fly through stone walls," said Paul, "What we do is decided by a greater power. Not by our choice."

"But there is a way out from the House," Adam Blackwood admitted.

"There is?"

"What man would build such a House without a sally-port?" John Traquair declared.

"Then why?" asked Amy, "has her Majesty been confined here?"

"Milady," Mary said, dropping her eyes, "it would not be proper for a lady in her condition."

"The sally," Adam Blackwood confessed, "is from the lang drop."

"The lang drop?"

"I think," said Paul, "Adam means the loo."

"The gardez-loo," Adam agreed.

Amy said, "A royal flush!"

She began to laugh although Mary Seton was deeply embarrassed.

Paul sighed, "Trust us to land in the…"

John Traquair pulled open the narrow door revealing the primitive lavatory, the chaise percee and the house-high drop into the shallow stream running under the foundations down to the Jedwater. The stale odour of human waste drifted upward.

Looking at its narrow dimensions, Amy agreed, "No way could her Majesty have got down there."

"We come out at the Jed?" Paul asked.

"No," Adam Blackwood replied, "The sally runs up into the town."

"Thank the Lord for that," Paul prayed, "I wasn't looking forward to crawling down a sewer."

The knotted rope tumbled down the shaft splashing into the water below.

"One for the money, two for the show," sang Paul, "Three to get ready and go, cat, go!"

Paul held the rope tightly and followed Adam Blackwood down into the darkness as Amy followed behind him.

*

Mary Stuart, Queen Regnant of Scotland, awoke when the baby, the past and future King James the Sixth of Scotland, the First of England, began to cry.

She struggled to sit up as Joyce Bowman and Tina, carrying a tea tray, entered the bedroom.

"His Royal Highness is very prompt, your Majesty," Joyce said, taking the tray from Tina who curtsied to the Queen, recited, "Majesty!" and picked the baby from his cot. Joyce put the tray on the bedside table. Gathered into Tina's embrace, James stopped crying.

"Ah!" said the Queen, "You are his favourite! He will not be quiet for me and I am his Sovereign."

"He knows he will be fed, Majesty," Tina said, "It's only cupboard love."

Mary laughed and repeated the phrase, "Cupboard love. I like it. Cupboard love."

Tina recited, "Majesty," curtseyed, and cuddling the baby, left the bedroom.

"Tina is not the wet nurse, no?" Mary asked, gesturing that perhaps Tina's slim figure was inadequate for the task.

Joyce said, "No, no, we have the admirable Mistress Cowengate to thank. But Tina is a very good nursemaid. James is in the safest hands."

"Then you must give the good woman my thanks. And silver, perhaps, when we leave?"

The doctor plumped up the Queen's pillows and settled her to sit up in bed. In Amy's bed, she thought, *39, Wellington Terrace, Gosforth. How quickly the unbelievable has become my reality.* She slipped the thermometer into the royal mouth and took the pale thin wrist to count her pulse.

"You're a very good patient, Majesty," Joyce commented as she withdrew the thermometer and completed her chart.

"I have much to thank you for. I owe my life to you."

Joyce said, "I suspect you're ready for a cup of tea?"

"Tea-time," the Queen cried, "I have grown to look forward to tea-time. It is tea-time?"

"Yes, Majesty, it is tea-time."

"Please pour yourself a cup of tea-time. We will sit together and share tea-time."

Joyce poured and milked two cups of her mother's willow pattern crockery and they sat together drinking tea and nibbling tuna sandwiches. Mary had become accustomed to this odd habit of hiding tidbits between two slices of bread. On the bed lay the Queen's handiwork, the unfinished embroidery; *In My End is My Beginning.*

"It is a strange country this Gosforth of yours."

"In what way, Majesty?"

"I hear all manner of strangeness."

Joyce braced herself to answer questions, which if answered honestly, would provoke a thousand more. She prepared herself to lie brazenly. *Why isn't Derek here? The man's a supreme liar. Nobody thinks faster on his feet than Derek, damn him!*

"What sort of strangeness, Majesty?"

"Of thunder and roaring creatures."

Joyce crossed her fingers and suggested, "Gosforth is a terrible place for thunder, Majesty."

"Still I have unravelled one mystery."

With dread in her heart the good doctor asked, "Yes? What would that be?"

With some satisfaction Mary announced, "This house is on the shore."

"How do you know, Majesty?"

Mary smiled and wagged a finger at Joyce.

"Aha, I am right! Night and day I hear the surf pounding on the beach. Am I right?"

Joyce thought of the endless rumbling of the central motorway running through the city and nodded agreement.

"You are right, Majesty. A safe house. A short walk from the shore."

"But in all this time," the Queen mused, "I have never heard a horse."

"A horse?" said Joyce, struggling for salvation. *Of course, she comes from a world of horses! And streets deep in horse.*

"I have said to myself. What is it that is so strange here? I listen and I listen. Strange! I hear no horses. Are there no horses in Gosforth?"

Mary looked enquiringly at Joyce in whose head the hamster was racing madly on the treadmill.

Reluctantly, but truthfully, she said, "That is because there are no horses."

The Queen was astonished.

"How can that be? No horses? How can there be no horses?"

The hamster fell off the treadmill.

"The household," said Joyce hesitantly, "has orders not to disturb his Royal Highness. Nor you, Majesty."

Mary nodded understanding.

Joyce continued, truthfully, "No horses are to be brought near the house. Straw has been laid everywhere. You have been so ill."

She was thankful for the fragment of memory of reading straw was laid in the streets outside hospitals during World War One.

157

Mary, Queen of Scots, smiled and said, "I shall not forget how kind you have been to me and my son."

And devious, thought Joyce, saying aloud, "No problem, Majesty."

"No problem?"

"No problem is without a solution, Majesty," said Joyce, surprised at her ingenuity.

Tea-time was finished, tea and tuna devoured.

Mary said, "I wish to sleep."

The doctor settled her pillows and straightened her coverlet. When she stood up she saw the Queen was already asleep. Which was not surprising, considering what Doctor Bowman prescribed in the royal teacup. Joyce picked up the needlework and read aloud, "In my end is my beginning," and folded it away. "Whatever that means."

As if on cue Tina entered with the baby, satisfied, sanitary and somnolent. His Royal Highness settled happily into his cot. The lights were diminished to a night-light, Joyce and Tina exchanged whispers. Tina settled into the bedside chair and Joyce, raising a hand in salute, left the bedroom. She knew as she walked downstairs no evil creature would approach mother and child so long as Tina was on watch. In this strangest of situations Joyce felt an echo of happiness.

*

In that moment when Margaret Lennox sprang about to confront the detective, Derek Bowman knew they were both about to die. Surprise lost, Susan stood irresolute. Derek strained against his invisible bonds and the witch laughed, saying, "Struggle if you wish, little fish! But you are well netted."

Susan stumbled a half step from Margaret Lennox and began to whimper. What Susan saw Derek couldn't see, but whatever apparition the witch presented held the young woman petrified with terror.

"Leave her alone!" Derek cried, "Let her go! You have me! Torture me, kill me, but let her go!"

As he pleaded with the Countess he felt again the bonds slacken and he began to dig his heels and elbows into the bedding and push himself slowly towards the woman, finding more freedom the more he begged for Susan's life.

"You have no quarrel with her! I'm the father of the twins! Let her go! She doesn't understand what's going on. But I do! I'm your enemy!"

Suddenly he found himself within reach and drawing up his legs he kicked at the witch catching her as she turned to him, throwing her off-balance. Momentarily, the spell was broken and Susan, waking, seized the moment and struck the witch in the face with the heavy vase, which burst in an explosion of splinters. Margaret Lennox tottered, tried to speak and crumpled to the floor. Derek climbed off the bed as Susan flung herself into his embrace and began to sob wildly. Derek struggled to calm the young woman.

"It's over," he soothed her, "She's done. You were stronger than she was. It was all smoke and mirrors! She wasn't real!"

Derek stirred the form on the floor, his shoe breaking through the moldering fabric releasing an appalling stink that made them step back. Among the shards of pottery there were only dusty rags and long-dead bones. The skull crumbled to fragments when Derek put a foot to it.

"Of course," said Derek Bowman, "you'll have to pay for the vase you broke."

Susan began to laugh. She sat on the bed and wiped away her tears.

"I'm sorry," she said, "Making a fool of myself."

"It's only natural," Derek suggested, "After all, you're only a feeble woman."

"When I find another vase," Susan suggested and pulled the counterpane from the bed.

"What're you doing?"

"Before the next turn takes the stage we need to take all this," she said, indicating the pathetic remains of Margaret, Countess of Lennox, "and burn it in the garden. Make an end of it, once and for all."

Derek helped Susan gather every last fragment into the counterpane. When he stood up, she said, "There's a cat. Or what looked like a cat. In my room. I bashed it with the vase."

Derek stepped back and, in admiration, said, "Wow! Atta girl! Let's go get it."

The fragments of the cat suitably bagged they parted on the threshold to Susan's room as she said, "One down, two to go. This alternative universe may be in retreat, but it ain't dead yet! Let's get out of here."

Derek said, "I'll go steal the towels."

Susan turned back to her room to recover her belongings while Derek went to retrieve his overnight bag. When Susan came out onto the landing again she heard footsteps begin to ascend the stairs.

SIXTEEN

Paul extended a hand to pull Amy up from the exit to the House sally port. Looking about them in the stables of the Spread Eagle, they dusted each other down. All the stalls were empty except for two chestnut hacks. Adam Blackwood returned from the stable doors.

"There are two carriages in the yard. And two liveries. One is the King's and the other, I fancy, is the Countess of Lennox."

Raised voices in the yard drew them to the stable doors. Her maids were assisting a richly dressed woman with a sour face into an open carriage. Her escort formed about for the journey. From the inn door, bowed out by the obsequious innkeeper and flunkeys came the man, Paul and Amy, assumed must be Lord Darnley, the petit roi. Among his attending bodyguard, he seemed slight and effeminate; his voice shrill and petulant. He slapped the page who helped him into his carriage.

"Well," decided Paul, "if we're going to do it."

The trio opened the stable door and walked towards the carriages. Immediately a shout went up from the escort and halberdiers ran to bar their way.

To the officer, Adam Blackwood said, "We come under parley from the House. On her Majesty's behalf, we are here to petition the King."

"And your office, sir?" enquired the officer.

"Adam Blackwood, Writer to her Majesty."

The officer indicated Paul and Amy.

"They are confidantes to the Queen. They have alarming news to share with his Majesty."

"How fares the Queen?" asked Lord Darnley without any display of concern.

"Considering the circumstances," Adam Blackwood replied, "Her Majesty is not in ultimate distress."

"I am much relieved," said his royal personage.

You pompous little squirt, thought Paul, *I'd love to give you a punch in the gob!*

"And who are these persons?" the Countess demanded.

Amy curtsied and said, "Milady, we would like to…"

"Did I ask you to speak?" interrupted the Countess.

"They have her Majesty's confidence," Adam Blackwood countered, "English gentry. If it please you, may I present Lady Amy and Lord Paul?"

"Of Gosforth," Paul added.

"What do English want here? More of that woman's papish tricks?"

She really does hate Mary, thought Amy, *so much poison in so few words.*

"We wish to petition his Majesty."

"And to warn him."

The petit roi said, "We will hear the petition."

Amy said, "Your Majesty, your wife, the Queen, is besieged in the House by the Earl of Bothwell. She is close to bearing your child."

Lord Darnley turned his head away and Amy was filled with the utmost loathing for this pygmy of a man.

Margaret Lennox said, "His Majesty will not hear your petition. What of this warning?"

Amy could not bring herself to speak.

Paul said, "When Bothwell has murdered your wife and child, sir, he will come to Edinburgh and kill you, your Majesty."

Lord Darnley shrank away, but the Countess of Lennox struck Paul with her cane and as he staggered under the blow, struck him again.

"Your stick will not save him," Paul countered.

The gentlemen of the escort half-drew their swords, but desisted when Adam Blackwood pulled Paul away.

Amy cried, "His Majesty will die at Kirk o' Field."

For one unforgettable moment Amy saw abject terror in Lord Darnley's face and then his carriage, escorted by his bodyguard, rattled away.

"Should that happen, mistress," Margaret Lennox warned, "I will look for you and I will find you!"

At a nod from the Countess, her carriage drew away, bodyguard buzzing as a swarm of wasps.

Watching the carriages depart the inn yard Amy lamented, "We've failed."

Adam Blackwood said, "Perhaps he has to die so that other good may prevail?"

"The little rat gets what he deserves," said Paul, holding a scarf to his bleeding face.

Adam Blackwood admitted, "The Countess is very ambitious for her son," Amy said, "When her son was murdered, Margaret Lennox blamed Mary. She has besieged the House for five hundred years."

Even as the three young people moved to return to the sally port a clatter of hooves alarmed them. Into the inn yard rode three men-at-arms. The leader cried, "Our mistress has a last message for you. Which we are charged to deliver."

Swords unsheathed, they trotted at Amy, Paul and Adam. Blades flashed in the air and the horsemen laughed as the victims scurried wildly to escape. There was nowhere to flee. Paul pulled Amy behind him and picked up a pitchfork. Adam Blackwood made a desperate lunge at a stirrup to pull the man down and staggered back, blood pouring from his head. The pitchfork was chopped from Paul's hands. There was nothing now between the twins and the raw blade. Paul pushed Amy behind him and turned a defiant face towards the horseman. Even as he heard the susurration of the crossbow bolts that sprouted suddenly from the chests of two horsemen, Paul saw the amputated hand that held the sword fly from the arm of the third man.

The horseman screamed as he was pulled him from the saddle and a sword sank to the hilt in his chest.

There was silence in the yard. Three horses stamped and whinnied nervously by three dead men. Amy became aware that John Traquair and two crossbowmen had followed them through the sally.

"Quickly, milady!" urged the Queen's Captain, "To the sally port afore they learn their loss!"

*

The footsteps climbed the stairs steadily, paused for a moment on the lower landing, but continued upward. Susan ran across the landing to Derek's room.

"Derek!" she said, "There's someone coming."

But there was no Derek and she fled across the landing to her own room. Holding the door open to the merest slit, she waited, watching the stairs to the landing. A bearded man, wearing a polo neck sweater, leather jacket and trousers, stepped cautiously onto the landing. Susan recognised him immediately. It was James Hepburn, Earl of Bothwell, the man on the CCTV from the charity shop. For a moment Susan thought he heard her sharp intake of breath.

Bothwell crossed to Derek Bowman's room and opened the door. He closed it and began to walk towards Susan's door. As he approached, Susan felt close to panic. The toilet flushed in the bathroom. Bothwell stopped. He returned to the stairs. With one last look around, he vanished from sight. As Derek emerged from the bathroom, Susan flew to him.

"Bothwell's just been here. The quicker we're out of here the better!"

As they approached the lower landing, the first smoke drifted upwards. From the landing they saw the hallway was an impassable sea of flame.

Susan said, "The bastard! He knew we were in the house."

She threw the improvised sack into the blaze.

Derek Bowman said, "What now? A helicopter?"

Susan took the large jardinière from its stand and hurled it through the landing window. The damage was impressive. The whole rainbow of Victorian images collapsed.

"You'll have to pay for that," warned Derek.

"Oooh, you got me scared now," Susan said and used the jardinière stand to clear the glass from the window frame. They looked down on a sloping slate roof and beyond, darkness.

"I'll go first," she announced, "Slide down the roof. Drop into the rhubarb. Easy peasy!"

The fire dragon roared in the hallway, but Derek hesitated. Susan said, "Chuck, chuck, chuck, chuck, chicken!" climbed out onto the slates, slid away and vanished into the garden.

"Come on in! The water's lovely!"

Derek climbed out of the window warily, shut his eyes, slid down the slates and landed in a cold frame with a shattering of glass.

As they climbed over the back fence, they heard the fire engine and stood for a moment to watch its arrival.

Derek said, "That creature, the woman, said, Elizabeth is at Newcastle on the Tyne. So near and yet so far. But they shall not succeed! They will believe Elizabeth has departed. But a broken axle holds her in Newcastle yet. I don't know what it means, but it must be important. Paul and Amy don't know this."

"Right! We go to the House and pass the news."

"But how?" asked Derek Bowman.

"You will tell them," said Susan, "You will tell your son and daughter. Let them work out what it means."

*

"You look like a Musselman," said John Traquair and laughed, but Adam, head swathed in a turban of bandages, didn't find it amusing.

Amy looked reproachfully at Traquair.

"Without a weapon. Adam tried to pull down a horseman. He was very brave."

Adam Blackwood, mollified, said, "I acted out of instinct."

"I apologise," offered Traquair, "Where is that pigeon?"

Safely back in the House and freshly dressed, they had been informed that a carrier had alighted in the pigeon loft carrying a message from Mary's agent in Newcastle. Even as Traquair spoke a houseman ran up the stairs to the outer chamber, bowed and presented him with a tiny curl of paper. The Captain took the message into the light of the lamp. From the stained fragment of paper, he read out the words, "She has come and waits until octobre end."

"She?" said Amy, "Who is this she?"

Adam Blackwood said, "Elizabeth of England, milady."

The twins exchanged glances.

Paul said, "I think it's time you told us what this is all about."

"You do not know?" an astonished Adam asked.

"You'd be surprised how little we know," Amy admitted.

"There has been a secret negotiation," Adam confessed, "Elizabeth has come to Newcastle to sign the Concordance of Newcastle, reconciling the two monarchs, stabilising the two kingdoms. Preparing for the Union of Scotland and England under the dual crown of Mary and Elizabeth."

"But that isn't in the history books," Amy protested, "I've never heard of it!"

"Because," Paul declared, "it never happened. They never met. Because Bothwell carried off the Queen, murdered Darnley, forced her to marry him, thereby alienating both Elizabeth and the Scottish nobles. That's why it didn't happen. So the inevitable progress to Fotheringhay and the block began."

"But they must meet!" Amy protested, "This will change everything! Don't you see, Paul? This is why we're here. To see it does happen."

"Til October ends," recited Paul, "What's today's date, Adam?"

"Today is the second of November."

"Why didn't he launch the pigeon sooner?" Amy lamented.

John Traquair said, "I have no doubts he did, milady. But this is not the pigeon's season. He has been perched in a tree. Sitting out the rain. Yet he'll make you a fine pie."

Amy was distressed.

"Oh, no, please, don't do that! I'm sure the poor thing has done his best."

"A poor best, milady. If the message is correct, Elizabeth has left Newcastle."

"Then all our efforts are for nothing."

*

Derek Bowman parked the Hummer by the railings of the Jethart House. When they climbed out into the rain, they were relieved to see a light in a lower window. The heavy door was locked.

"Maybe there's a door in Jedburgh where somebody answers?" suggested Derek and rapped sharply on the sturdy oak.

"Just so long as it isn't another zombie," Susan said.

Derek rapped again and they heard footsteps approaching. When Angus Fleckie opened the door relief was apparent on all three faces.

Angus said, "You never know whether you should open the door after dark."

"Then you remember us?" Susan asked.

"Oh, my word, yes! Come along in!"

Angus appeared genuinely pleased to see Susan and Derek.

The heavy door closed behind them and they moved into the guard chamber where Angus had papers spread out on the Reception desk under the light.

"You're lucky to find me here. But I thought tonight, I'll settle myself down and clear some of the paperwork. Oh, my word, you'd be surprised how many forms the House has to complete. So many questions to be answered to persuade eminent bodies to part with the smallest grant to keep our door open."

He pushed his glasses up his nose and smiled at them, "But I'm babbling on, aren't I? How can I help you?"

Derek Bowman took out his wallet and counted out bank notes on to the desk as Angus's eyes opened wide.

"Count this, "said Derek, "as a small donation to help keep the House door open."

"Oh, my word!" said Angus, "How kind!"

"If you would simply allow us to stand in the upper chamber," Susan said, "We'd be very grateful. We won't touch anything. But this is the last place Mr. Bowman's children visited before..."

"I understand," said Angus, "I did read of the tragedy," and to Derek, "Please feel free. Give me half a minute and I'll put the lights on for you."

"You're very kind," Derek said, "Thank you."

They walked up the stairs together.

"A very decent young man," Derek commented.

"Oh, my word, yes!" Susan said and they laughed.

The upper chamber hushed them to silence. They stood in the silence until Derek said, "I don't know how to do this. I don't know how you can communicate with the past."

"If Bothwell and his ape," said Susan, "can intrude on us, then here is the place you may speak to your children. They're here. I know they are. This is where it began and this is where it will end."

It was Susan who saw the first shadow move. It was Derek who cried out as Amy appeared as simply as a flower opens. Beside her Paul grew out of shadow. No one spoke. Then Susan realised Derek Bowman was weeping.

When he started to move forward Susan restrained him. Before her unbelieving eyes the image changed. The teenagers in shirt, jeans and nightdress became a young man and woman in Stuart dress. The young woman's clothing was particularly opulent. *A young queen*, thought

Susan, *my God, I'm looking at a queen.*

Susan said, "The queen. Elizabeth. She's still in Newcastle. A broken axle. I think this is important for you to know."

Then they were gone. As an electric light is switched off. Susan and Derek were alone in the upper chamber. Susan waited as the teenagers' father composed himself. *If I live to be a hundred,* Susan thought, *no one will ever believe what I have seen.*

To Derek Bowman, she said, "We've done all we can do. What happens now has nothing to do with us. Let's fall into the monster and go home to Newcastle."

Derek Bowman nodded agreement and they walked down the stairs in silence.

Angus Fleckie was standing at the Reception desk.

"I hope everything was satisfactory?"

Derek said, "Yes, thank you. That was all we needed."

Angus handed over a slip of paper to Derek Bowman.

"Your receipt. For your donation. We'll put it to good use."

Derek folded the receipt and pushed it into a pocket.

Susan said, "Thank you, Angus. We'll hit the road now."

Derek turned to open the great oak door and found it locked.

"It's locked."

"One can't be too careful," said Angus and came to open the door.

Derek stepped back and Angus, to Susan's total astonishment, stabbed him in the side.

"My God!" cried Derek Bowman and collapsed to the floor, hands reaching for his wound. Angus turned to Susan, a long stiletto in his hand. The young woman stared bewildered at the smiling young man. *No one is who they seem to be*, thought Susan, *More fool me! We'll both die here in this damned House.*

She backed away as Angus advanced upon her, desperately seeking a weapon. Then she saw Derek Bowman struggling to drag himself after the assassin, but Angus smiled and turned to stamp on Bowman's hand. Yet the distraction was enough for Susan to snatch the fire extinguisher and strike their attacker on the side of his head. Angus fell forward onto his face and screamed. He lay still as Susan strove to regain her breath. Derek struggled to prop himself up against the wall. Then Susan saw the blood pool spreading below Angus's still form. When she turned him over she saw he had fallen on the stiletto. There was no pulse and no heartbeat.

"He's dead."

"Better him than me," said Derek Bowman and winced.

"Does it hurt?"

"Only when I laugh," said Derek, watching the blood seep between his fingers.

"Ah, the old jokes are still the worst!" Susan commented, "Let's see if we can stop the bleeding."

Susan found the First Aid kit behind the Reception desk. She cleaned and dressed the stab wound.

"Fortunately you're fat," she said.

"How unkind!" Derek complained.

"I don't think he hit any vital organ. Not very good at stabbing was our Angus, thank God."

"Oh, my word, no!" echoed Derek.

"I reckon you'll last until we can get you to Newcastle."

"With you driving?"

"Anything gets in my way," Susan declared, "is dead meat."

They stepped out into the sudden darkness of night. The gnarled limbs of old pear trees were eerily visible in the lamplight. Susan turned the antique key in the lock and dropped the keys into the letterbox mounted beside the door. They had left Angus lying where he lay, but cleaned and returned the fire extinguisher to its position.

They stepped back to look at the sinister bulk of the House, silhouetted against the streetlights.

"I wouldn't want to try to fight my way in there," Derek commented.

A sudden thought struck Susan.

"Why didn't Angus try to kill us before we passed on the message about Elizabeth?"

"Taken by surprise?"

Susan shook her head.

"He was ready for us. Knew we were coming. Bothwell is a clever bastard."

"If this news is important and Margaret Lennox thought so, then it's important to Amy and Paul," determined Derek Bowman.

"And Bothwell let us pass the news."

"Why would he do that?"

"To bring them out of the House. He doesn't want to fight his way in there either."

They were silent. Susan closed the gate and they walked to the Hummer. Derek surrendered the keys. They climbed in and locked safety belts.

Looking at the brooding cliff of the House Derek said, "I think we're spectators. No more to do. It all hangs in the balance now. Can you not feel it?"

"Yes," said Sally, "Everything is waiting. As if a storm were approaching."

Detective Constable Susan Duffy started the Hummer's engine and its owner said a quiet prayer.

*

"There's only one little difficulty, Amy," said Paul, "One minor detail. Mary isn't here! Without her the Concordance of Newcastle isn't going to happen."

Blackwood and Traquair nodded agreement.

"As it didn't happen," Paul added.

Amy said, as if repeating something overheard, "I will play the Queen."

Blackwood and Traquair looked to one another in astonishment.

Mary Seton said, "Oh, milady!"

"I will play the Queen," Amy repeated, "That is why I am here. That is what is meant to be."

The silence in the outer chamber was broken by the calling of the House sentries one to another: all posts secure.

"You have the look of the Queen, milady" John Traquair admitted.

Adam Blackwood suggested, "A little shorter in stature?"

"High heels will make up the difference," Amy declared.

"Who would dare stare at a Queen?" said Mary Seton.

"They have never met. Elizabeth and Mary," Paul said, "No one will question."

"Then we are agreed?" declared John Traquair.

*

As Joyce Bowman walked upstairs carrying cocoa to the Queen of Scotland she was startled and delighted to see her daughter Amy in Stuart dress hurrying downstairs towards her.

"Amy, what're you...?"

Amy waved three pairs of high-heeled shoes at her mother.

"Sorry, Mum, in a bit of a hurry. Explain later. Must fly! Thanks for the shoes!"

Amy vanished. Joyce Bowman stood on the stairs and steadied the mugs of cocoa on the tray.

To the empty air she said, "Have a good time, darling! Don't do anything I wouldn't do," and continued up the stairs to share cocoa and conversation with her friend, Mary Stuart.

*

"If we can get out of the House," said Paul, "How long would it take to reach Newcastle?"

"Two days in good weather, my lord," said Traquair, "if the Lady Amy rides. If she is to be carried in a litter three, four days."

"Why not a carriage?"

Adam Blackwood shook his head.

171

"To take a carriage over the Cheviots this time of year is not a task I'd envy anyone, my lord."

Amy said, "I'm sure I could sit on a horse."

"Two days on horseback in the rain?" Paul questioned his sister.

"Are you not forgetting Bothwell's levies?" suggested John Traquair, "Even if we should fight free of the House it's a long chase from here to the Tyne. They'll not give us a neighbourly hand to mount the Cheviots."

Paul looked to Amy. *We're losing them. The longer we delay. It's all or nothing. If this is what we were chosen to do then so be it. If we could pull it off, wouldn't it be great? Agreed? We go?*

Turning to Blackwood, Traquair and Mary Seton, Paul said, "We leave for Newcastle tonight."

Stifling their protests Paul continued, "The longer we delay the less will be any prospect of success. The Lady Amy and I are willing to take the chance. The prize is too great to delay. We leave tonight."

In the Queen's chamber Mary Seton and a maid prepared Amy for the journey in Mary's travelling dress. When the last ribbon was tied and the last button buttoned, Amy, balanced on her mother's high heels, pirouetted for inspection.

"Milady, I do declare you are sister to the Queen," cried an awed Mary Seton and the maid mutely agreed.

"If we are bold," Mary Seton continued, "We shall carry it off."

"How would Mary address Elizabeth?" Amy wondered.

"As she writes," Mary Seton offered, "calling her sister."

"I trust she turns out to be so," said Amy, "I will be in her hands."

"The policies have all been agreed. All you may need to perform is to sign the parchment."

"Show me her signature," Amy said.

A plan for the breakout was drawn up by John Traquair. The escapers, to Amy's horror, would crawl, wrapped in sackcloth, through the primitive sewer to the Jedwater and wait, hidden under the lip of the riverbank. A force of halberds and archers would be sent through the sally to the Spread Eagle and attack the encamped reivers from the flank to draw them off from the House. When the diversion was well under way horses, primed with salt water, would be released from the House. They would instinctively stampede to the river. The reivers left to cover the House would see only riderless horses, but bowmen would also sally out to keep the besiegers at bay and cover the flight of the horses.

The nightmare began. Claustrophobic Amy, huddled in sackcloth, squeezed through the sewer on hands and knees, following a terrified maidservant, Jane, who followed on the boot heels of Adam Blackwood who crawled after John Traquair. Mary Seton followed Amy. Paul brought up the rear.

When the maid swooned in the sewer, the enterprise was in grave danger. The two men in front reached the riverbank only to realise no one was following. John Traquair crawled back into the sewer to find Amy and Mary Seton suffocating behind the unconscious maid. With great difficulty Traquair pulled the girl, Jane, free and released the rest of the party.

However, the attackers from the Spread Eagle were unaware of the near disaster in the sewer and the timing was thrown out of joint. When the tumult was at its height, the horses were released. They galloped to the river to drink, wading into the stream. With Traquair in the sewer struggling to free the wretched maid, Adam Blackwood, alone, watched helplessly as reivers splashed into the water to catch the horses' reins, gleeful and triumphant.

When the escape party had finally assembled under the bank lip, exhausted and frightened, the horses had gone, ridden away by Bothwell's clansmen. All seemed to be lost. The sally party at the Spread Eagle retreated, leaving dead and wounded. The dispirited escapees huddled under a cold moon. But the uproar did not die down. Bothwell and his clansmen were triumphant; having forestalled a breakout, they sensed victory was near.

The celebration went on late into the night. The dispirited Queen's party lay on the riverbank and watched across the meadowland the enemy at their campfires. Return to the House was impossible. Amy couldn't bear the thought of entering again the slimy, suffocating passageway. If they trekked across country from where could they expect to find horses? They lay and listened to the uproar of song and laughter at the campfires.

"They believe the battle to be won," commented Adam Blackwood.

"Then we must undeceive them," John Traquair said, "Needs must when the Devil drives."

The three men left the women at the riverbank and crawled through the grass towards the horse lines. Campfires flared, throwing giant shadows. Noise, song and laughter from the triumphant reivers covered their movements. The three men gained the horse lines to find the horses from the House still saddled.

"Careless," whispered Adam Blackwood, "Someone might easy steal these nags."

Blackwood drifted away, merely a shadow, between two horses. Paul, not at ease with horses, struggled with a mare that resented being taken from her sister.

The mare neighed loudly, and fought Paul who struggled to lead her into the darkness. John Traquair brought up the rear, leading two horses. At the riverbank, Paul lost the mare. She galloped neighing towards the campfires and aroused the reivers to the loss of the horses. With shouts and war cries they came running towards the river. The maid, Jane, frightened, screamed and ran off into darkness. Amy and Mary Seton struggled to mount sidesaddle.

"What goes where?" Amy cried.

Paul, foolishly guilty, cried, "It's my fault! I lost the horse. I'll stay!"

Without a word, Paul was bundled onto horseback by John Traquair. Adam Blackwood leapt astride the last horse, stretching out a hand to pull the Captain aboard. But Traquair shook his head, crying, "Be away! God speed!"

The last Paul and Amy saw of the gallant Captain as they splashed across the Jedwater, was John Traquair standing foursquare to face the onrushing enemy, sword in hand. Then they were among the trees and branches slashed at their faces as they rode like the Devil himself towards the dark shoulders of the Cheviots.

*

They walked the winded horses up the stony track to where Carter Bar would-be-had-been-yesterday-tomorrow when the owl flew across their path. Their mistake was not understanding what drove the bird. It was of little consequence as there was nowhere to run and hide.

As they came over the shoulder they stopped to draw breath before descending towards England, and the city on the Tyne where the Queen of England slept in her own bed in a chamber decorated with her own hangings. Amy's thoughts were with brave John Traquair now dead on the gravel of the Jedwater. Even as she turned to speak to Paul their journey came to its untimely end.

From the shadow of the rocks stepped James Hepburn, Earl of Bothwell, and Cymian, his dwarf. The bolt struck Adam Blackwood knocking him down even as he reached to draw his sword. At Cymian's shriek of triumph the horses whinnied and reared in terror with Paul hanging on desperately to reins he must not lose. *This time I won't let go!* Yet he was dragged from the path, struggling to contain the horses. Adam struggled to rise, clasping his shoulder.

Mary Seton, regardless of her own safety, rushed to him, dropping to her knees.

Amy stood aghast, paralysed, and moved off the path into the heather as Cymian motioned with his crossbow.

"Go ahead," Amy cried, "Kill a girl. You're quite a hero!"

The dwarf reloaded his crossbow.

"Be not in such haste, milady," declared Bothwell.

"There's no deal you can make with us," Paul said, "Mary is beyond your reach. And the baby lives."

Cymian swivelled the crossbow to threaten the young man holding the restive horses.

"Perchance I should kill your brother first?"

Amy answered, defiantly, "How would that serve you? The game is played out. You won't get your hands on the Queen and the baby."

"That may be," said Bothwell, "but she is not here to claim her crown. You think to play games with me? You have played and lost. When you die here you are truly dead."

The dwarf aimed at Amy's breast.

"Mary and her squealing ween are shipwrecked. And will never come home again. She will end up in a madhouse."

Bothwell nodded towards Amy.

"Kill her!"

Then, out of nowhere, visible only for the blinking of an eye, a monstrous machine roared over the crest and struck Bothwell and

Cymian: like a lightning flash in a thunderstorm, seen and unseen in a heartbeat: master and servant, vanished over the edge of the precipice screaming, falling to die on the rocks below.

*

Derek Bowman checked for messages on his mobile as the Hummer, driven by the detective constable, passed the border stone and the car entered the time anomaly. For the briefest of moments, Susan Duffy saw everything clearly: a man on his knees clutching a bloody shoulder, a woman kneeling beside him, a young man clinging to the reins of two wild-eyed horses, the man she knew as Bothwell and a young woman facing the dwarf's crossbow. As the bolt flew, Susan Duffy stamped on the accelerator. The bolt ricocheted from the Hummer as the car struck Bothwell and the dwarf. The thwack, thwack as the broken bodies were thrown aside was loud in the driver's ears. Susan brought the car to a rubber-burning halt.

"What happened?" asked Derek Bowman, fumbling for his mobile phone in the footwell, wincing at the pain from his wound.

Susan Duffy, looking into the rear view mirror, saw an empty road behind her.

"I've just killed Bothwell and his dwarf."

Derek Bowman looked at her blankly.

"Stay there," said Susan and climbed out of the Hummer.

The young detective constable walked round to examine the bull bars.

"What're you looking for?"

Susan walked back up to the border stone, searching the road verges.

When she returned to the Hummer Derek Bowman asked, "Satisfied?"

"Never more so," Susan smiled.

"Then d'y'think you could get me to a hospital before I bleed to death? I've been stabbed, y'know!"

Susan climbed into the driver seat.

"How're you going to explain being stabbed with a sixteenth century stiletto?"

SEVENTEEN

In the silence of his familiar room Paul woke out of a sound sleep, vivid dreams fading beyond recall. He lay listening to his sister Amy singing and showering in the bathroom next door. When he swung his feet to the Mickey Mouse mat the alarm clock began to buzz. As ever he took an especial delight in slapping it into silence. Knuckles rapped on the door and his mother's voice declaimed, "Are you vertical, Paul, or shall I come in and embarrass you?"

In the bathroom the shower and singing stopped.

"I'm up, Mum, I'm up," Paul declared, and reached for his dressing gown.

"You don't want to miss the coach, do you?" coaxed the voice from the landing.

When he opened the bedroom door his mother was retreating down the stairs and the bathroom door stood open. From the airing cupboard shelf Paul took a fresh towel and closed the bathroom door behind him. He was pleasantly surprised to find Amy hadn't sung away all the hot water.

Joyce Bowman switched on the radio as she moved to retrieve the toast that had jumped from the toaster to the kitchen floor. *Why does it always do that to me? It never does that to Amy!* Reproving Joyce Bowman, the newsreader declared, "The Minister ended by saying we must all take responsibility for our actions and not blame technical deficiencies."

"Shame on me," Joyce Bowman said aloud and smiled. The newsreader paused from chiding Joyce Bowman to continue brightly with:

"At eleven o'clock this morning the Prime Minister of Great Britain, David Traquair, will meet the Prime Minister of Ireland mid-way beneath the Irish Sea for the ceremonial opening of the new Stranraer-Belfast Tunnel. The long-awaited Strunnel. The Irish Prime

Minister will accompany Mr. Traquair on his return to Edinburgh where Mister Doughty will be presented with the Freedom of the City. Both men will dine with the Queen at Holyrood House and tomorrow, Mister Doughty will address Parliament. Next weekend Mister Traquair will be the guest of the Irish Government in Belfast and Dublin."

As Joyce buttered her toast the newsreader declared in a reproving tone: "In London last night, a violent demonstration in support of a greater degree of self-government for the province of England was contained by firm police action. The Edinburgh Office has issued a statement that the Government would look favourably upon a greater degree of English autonomy. Although Birmingham is now the administrative capital of the province, London is the focal centre for the notorious English National Party. The First Ministers of Kernow and Wales have both stated their support for central Government."

The newsreader paused and continued in a brighter tone: "Production figures in the Scottish offshore oil industry last month showed an increase of seventeen point eight percent and the Royal Bank of Scotland said a decrease in the public sector borrowing requirement was responsible for. . ."

Amy entered the kitchen, switched off the radio, dropped bread into the toaster and kissed her mother.

"Good morning, Mother dear!"

"Good morrow, Offspring of my loins!"

"Mum!" cried Amy, "It's too early in the morning for loins!"

The toaster clicked, Amy caught the flying toast and sat down to butter and crunch with almost balletic grace.

Aren't I lucky to have such a daughter? thought Joyce Bowman.

"Is Paul up?"

Amy swallowed toast and said, "In the shower. Where's Dad?"

"Out on his run."

"He's promised us a lift."

Joyce Bowman consulted her wrist.

"About now he'll be staggering down Culloden Terrace. If he doesn't have a heart attack between there and home he'll take you,"

Joyce reassured her daughter, "If he has a heart attack I'll take you. We'll pop him in the boot."

178

Amy swallowed the last crumbs of her toast, gulped down half a cup of tea and vanished into the hallway to collect her bag and coat.

"Do come on, Paul!" Amy shouted up the stairs.

Her mother followed Amy out into the hallway.

"They won't keep the coach waiting just for you two!"

"I'm ready to go!" said Paul, coming down the stairs.

"You've had no breakfast," his mother complained.

"I'm not hungry."

"We've got our packed lunches," Amy assured her mother.

The front door opened and Derek Bowman, red of face and short of breath, stumbled in.

His wife said, "Ah, good! You didn't have a heart attack?"

Amy asked anxiously, "Are you sure this running is doing you good, Dad?"

"A doctor," said Derek Bowman M.D., "should set an example to his patients."

"By dropping dead from a heart attack?" suggested Paul, "Right on!"

His father laughed.

"Why the delegation?"

"Because you're giving your offspring a lift to school? The Field Trip?"

"Oh, suckaboo! I'd forgotten! Is that today?"

The teenagers and their mother regarded each other in mock despair.

"Where did you get him from, Mum?" asked Amy.

Paul added, "Are you sure he is our father?"

"Where're you going?" asked their father ignoring the slurs cast on his mental stability.

"Jedburgh," said Paul, colliding with Amy's, "York."

Amy stared at her brother.

"Why would we go to Jedburgh?"

Why did I say Jedburgh?

"Like father, like son," said Amy to her mother and to her brother, "Wake up, Paul, we're going to York. Remember? York. Where Mary I of Scotland was crowned Mary II of England? The joint sovereignty of Mary and Elizabeth?"

"Was she?" Paul said, struggling to clear his head.

His father said, "You haven't been at the whacky baccy, have you?"

"Derek!" his wife cried, outraged.

"He just never listens," Amy excused him.

Paul struggled to catch strands of memory as fleeting as summer clouds and failed.

"Then they signed the Concordance of Newcastle?"

"Attaboy!" cried Amy, "Keep it up and you're Highers A star in History is assured."

"I was never much cop at History," her father declared, "History's made up by the winners."

"Thanks, Dad! That's a big help," said Amy, and to her brother, "Are you awake now, brother dear?"

The last time we were in Jedburgh we were children, weren't we?

Holiday in that awful caravan. Remember?

I remember you cut your foot wading after minnows.

Dad insisted on barbecuing those trout and they tasted disgusting.

They tasted okay to me.

They would! You'd eat anything.

As autumn leaves quit the tree the last shadows of images and voices drifted away.

"I'll see he gets on the right coach, Mum," Amy assured her mother.

"Don't I get time to change?" Derek Bowman complained.

"You've got a spare suit at the surgery," his wife reminded him.

Amy opened the front door onto a sunny Graham Park Road.

"Let's go!"

Derek kissed his wife affectionately.

"Yuck!" cried Paul, "Don't do that! I'm a sensitive child!"

"Be glad," his sister rebuked him, "you've got old-fashioned parents who live in the same house."

"Just take care of each other," their mother advised, "and come home safely."

"What about me?" asked Derek Bowman.

"So long as you use the back door."

Joyce Bowman closed the front door slowly and stood in the silent hallway smiling to herself.

"Old-fashioned parents who live in the same house," she said aloud and laughed at the simplicity of happiness. Later in the afternoon Joyce Bowman was to be inaugurated as the Chairperson of SPEAK, the organisation that safeguards the health and employment rights of Scottish women journalists. Her main concern today was to choose the right dress for the occasion and to practice her already well-practiced speech of acceptance.

In the silent sitting room a ginger cat watched the departure of the Mondeo from the windowsill. On the sofa lay a cushion. Beneath a faded coat of arms were the words *In my End is my Beginning* embroidered in gold and silver thread. The cat jumped down from the windowsill to settle on the cushion.

*

Polly McKenzie stood in the yard of Binny Farm and watched the open doors of the garage anxiously. The familiar rear of Morris Traveller FMY675G emerged, was smartly reversed and halted by Polly. A young man climbed out of the driver's seat.

"There yah, Mizz McKenzie," he said cheerily, "No problem."

"Thank you very much, John, What would I do without you?"

John smiled and said, "You'd get somebody else to back out the Morris?"

"You're too honest, John," Polly admitted and smiled.

"I'll be away then. Just leave her in the yard and I'll see to her."

As the young man turned to go, Polly said, "Have we done with the fifty acre yet?"

"Stan says we should finish today. Then we'll start on the Tangle tomorrow."

When the young man departed, Polly McKenzie looked to the house, checked her watch and went to stand in the open door of the farmhouse.

"Muriel! Whatever are you doing, girl! We're going to be late."

As if her sister had been awaiting the summons, Muriel McKenzie came down the staircase and walked past her sister towards the Morris.

"You didn't back the car out, did you?"

"I was going to, but John was in the yard. He insisted."

Muriel looked reproachfully at her sister.

"You're a very poor liar, Polly."

"Are you getting in or not?"

Polly started the engine and engaged first gear. The car began to roll forward towards the gate.

"I've changed my mind," said Muriel.

"We've made an appointment."

"It's stopped hurting."

"Teeth always stop hurting when one makes a dental appointment."

Polly engaged second gear and the Morris ran down the green-canopied lane.

"We'd be wasting Mr. Pruitt's time."

"We're paying for his time."

The Morris stopped at the junction with the Edinburgh road and turned towards Jedburgh.

"I believe I need the toilet," said Muriel, "Most immediately."

"I'm sure Mr. Pruitt has adequate toilet accommodation."

The Morris Traveller rolled steadily towards Jedburgh at thirty-eight mph, gathering a growing convoy behind her.

"You are a very cruel person," Muriel McKenzie decided, "I shall not speak to you again. I disown you as my sister."

"There is," said her disowned sister, "a certain satisfaction in driving certain persons to a dental appointment."

*

In the Reception area of the Queen's House in Jedburgh, Mary MacDonald discussed with her faithful Angus who would lead the groups booked into the House today. Angus would always remember when a gray-haired woman visited his school to explain how she had fought to restore the Queen's House to its former glory. After school, driven by curiosity, he had gone to the House and Mary MacDonald had showed him how she had marked and numbered every piece of stone so that each would be returned to its rightful place. From that moment on, Angus Fleckie became her willing slave.

"Perhaps if you were to take the Primary school group, Angus? You're so very good with the children."

"Whatever you say, Miss MacDonald."

Never would he have admitted how children frightened him with their inclination to drift away as he struggled to hold the group together. It was like trying to carry water in bare hands.

"Do emphasise it was from this House that Mary Stuart made her bid for freedom and fled to Newcastle to meet Elizabeth. We may not have the riches of Edinburgh Castle, but we represent a unique moment in our national history."

"Yes, Miss MacDonald."

"By all means show the children the woodcut of Earl Bothwell's body being hanged, drawn and quartered after his death on Carter Bar, but, please, don't take Bothwell's mummified hand from the display for children to shake. We've had three complaints of nightmares."

"No, Miss MacDonald."

"Would you check we have sufficient tea bags and Kit-Kats for the O.A.P.s? We could work together this afternoon?"

"Absolutely!"

"But I think it wiser not to demonstrate the crossbow? Mister Milligan has not forgiven us for what we did to his weathercock."

"He gave me an awful look yesterday."

"Oh, and once the children have gone, do cast an eye over the toilets?"

"Yes, Miss MacDonald."

"Could you do something with the lock on the Disabled Toilet? Although everyone applauded your forced entry through the window it was unfortunate the poor lady was trapped for an hour before anyone noticed she was missing."

In the quiet of this ancient House from which all clamour and clash of arms had long since departed a gray-haired spinster and a young man planned another working day.

*

Outside the gates of the Robert Bruce Academy the A Level History group foregathered to await the arrival of the coach. The popular and dedicated young teacher, David Griffiths, stood exchanging banter with envious scholars heading for another day in the classroom. His colleague, Nina Paice, a similarly enthusiastic historian, was talking with the girls. There was an air of excitement and expectation among teachers and students. When the Mondeo opened its doors to release Amy and Paul, both teachers smiled to greet the twins. Derek Bowman tapped the horn, the twins waved and the Mondeo swept away.

*

Detective Sergeant Susan Duffy parked the car behind the coach outside the Robert Bruce Academy. Two teachers, a man and a woman, were embarking students on to the coach. She unfastened her seat belt and turned to her passenger, Detective Constable John Timothy.

"Don't fall asleep. I might need you."

The Detective Constable said, "To frighten off parents from parking? In an unmarked police car?"

"Is that what we're doing here?" said Susan, seemingly surprised.

"Isn't that what you put on the job sheet?"

Susan looked at her colleague and shook her head sadly.

"I thought you knew me better than that by now."

"Then what're we doing here?"

Watching the last students climb aboard the coach, the Detective Sergeant said, "Any time now a BMW is going to park in front of us to let a kid out."

"And?"

"Driving it will be Harold Starling."

"Holey moley! You're kidding? The Harold Starling?"

"Drugs, prostitution, armed robbery, extortion, complicit in at least three murders. Anything evil going down in Newcastle, our Harold has a hand in it."

"But we've been trying to lift him for months! Every raid has come up blank."

"But what our elders and betters don't know," Susan explained, "is that Harold takes his daughter to school every morning."

She smiled at Timothy.

"A proud father who has deprived other children of their fathers."

"Wow!" said the Detective Constable, "And we get to lift him?"

"Got it in one!"

The coach pulled away from the kerb as a BMW slid in to take its place. The passenger door opened and a teenage girl exited, ran through the Academy gates and on towards the main building.

Duffy and Timothy were already out of the car and Susan was tapping on the driver's window as Timothy opened the passenger door. As the startled driver wound down his window Susan said, "Good morning, Harold! I am Detective Sergeant Duffy and I am arresting you on suspicion of causing or being implicated in the deaths of John Humphries, William Stanhope and Norman Taylor."

The surprised driver looked towards the D.C.'s handcuffs as Susan Duffy took the ignition keys.

"Krise sake, I'm taking my kid to school!" Harold Starling complained, "I mean, no way! This isn't bliddy fair!"

"I never play fair with scum," replied Detective Sergeant Susan Duffy.

*

In the coach, Amy and Paul sat together watching the city streets slide away as they drove south to the ancient city of York. The lead teacher, David Griffiths, moved down the aisle talking to his students. His colleague, Nina Paice, sat chatting with three girls in the back seat. The coach drove over the Tyne Bridge and the students glued their faces to the glass to gaze down on the familiar river. From the New Castle flew the cross of St. Andrew, the Scottish saltire. The same flag flew from St. Nicholas's Cathedral and the Tyne Bridge itself.

Diverting the course of history has a price. Like a stone thrown into a pool, the ripples spread far and wide.

THE END

Lest we lose touch with reality...

Mary, Queen of Scots, (1542 - 1587), was descended from Margaret Tudor, daughter of Henry VII, through her father King James V of Scotland. She became Queen of Scotland on the death of her father, a few days after her birth, and was regarded by many Catholics as the rightful Queen of England. In 1543, a treaty of betrothal was made between Mary and Edward (later Edward VI), son of Henry VIII.The Scottish nobles refused to recognise the treaty and five years later the infant queen was betrothed to the Dauphin of France, whom she married in 1558. While Mary was Queen of France, the Scottish Protestants, aided by Elizabeth I of England, overthrew the Catholic party in 1560. Consequently her arrival in Scotland in 1561, after the death of her husband, (Francis II) created a difficult position. This was not eased by her marriage in 1565 to her cousin, Henry, Lord Darnley, who, also a descendant of Margaret Tudor through his mother, the Countess of Lennox, had a claim to the English throne.

A rebellion of the nobles was crushed by Mary with the aid of James Hepburn, Earl of Bothwell. But her husband, Henry Darnley, angered at her refusal to grant him the crown, joined the opposition and headed the troop who murdered Rizzio, the Queen's secretary, adviser, and, quite possibly, her lover. Mary and Darnley were, however, reconciled for a brief time and their son, James, was born in 1566. But in the following year Bothwell headed a conspiracy which ultimately resulted in Darnley's death. Three months later the Queen married her husband's murderer after his trial and acquittal. Immediately, the nobles banded together and Mary was forced to separate from Bothwell, and then to yield herself prisoner and abdicate in favour of her son. After an abortive attempt to regain the throne she fled to England where she was kept in captivity by Elizabeth. In 1586 Mary was brought to trial for treason and executed on 8th February, 1587, in the hall of Fotheringhay Castle.